Alan Hunter was born in Hoveton, Norfolk in 1922. He left school at the age of fourteen to work on his father's farm, spending his spare time sailing on the Norfolk Broads and writing nature notes for the *Eastern Evening News*. He also wrote poetry, some of which was published while he was in the RAF during the Second World War. By 1950, he was running his own book shop in Norwich and in 1955, the first of what would become a series of forty-six George Gently novels was published. He died in 2005, aged eighty-two.

The *Inspector George Gently* series

Gently Down the Stream

Alan Hunter

ROBINSON

Constable & Robinson Ltd
3 The Lanchesters
162 Fulham Palace Road
London W6 9ER
www.constablerobinson.com

This paperback edition published by Robinson,
an imprint of Constable & Robinson Ltd, 2010

A copy of the British Library Cataloguing in Publication data is available
from the British Library

ISBN: 978-1-84901-500-4

Typeset by TW Typesetting, Plymouth, Devon

Printed and bound in the EU

1 3 5 7 9 10 8 6 4 2

FOR THE BOSUN
(my sister, E.M. Hunter)

and to the memory
of a peerless 16-foot sailing-dinghy

RECKLESS

CHAPTER ONE

THERE WAS SOMETHING wrong at Sloley's Yard. Everyone knew it, but nobody was sure what it was.

To start with, it had begun like every other Saturday morning during the high season. The men had come in early to begin clearing out the hire-boats which had drifted in on Friday night. A little later the women had come, chaffing and giggling, and soon the pillar-box red of boat blankets was seen as they were hung out to air in the hot June sun. Lastly came Old Man Sloley, white-bearded, neat in his old-fashioned slop-coat, and with him his son and junior partner, Harry, better known around the yard as young Rushm'quick. As usual, Old Man Sloley unlocked the office. As usual, young Rushm'quick set out in the long, low, powerful yard-launch to round up straggling hire-boats and, if necessary, tow them in. And for two hours, the work of preparation for a fresh batch of hirers went on without let or hindrance.

At the end of two hours, young Rushm'quick returned in the launch, an irritable expression on his face. He tossed the painter to a yard-hand, swore at him when he didn't catch it and strode off to the office at a high rate of knots. From the office could be heard the sound of the two partners in conference. Rushm'quick sounded exasperated and defensive, Old Man Sloley was plainly in his tantrums. In a short while Sid Seymour, who was innocently varnishing a gaff under the office window, reported that they were busy phoning round the yards and quarter of an hour later the yard foreman was summoned to the conference. He came out frowning.

'Fill up the launch – get the little tender out and fill her up, too.'

'Someth'n' wrong?' enquired Sid Seymour, who had dropped his gaff to attend to these orders.

'Never you mind. Just do what I tell you.'

Sid shrugged and went about his business. But he was pretty certain in his own mind now.

'They've lost a boat,' he muttered to Fidown Young. 'All this mystery about it!'

'Someone drowned, maybe . . .?' suggested Fidown hopefully.

'Drowned my foot! They'd've had the drags if it was a drowning job.'

But Fidown wasn't altogether convinced.

Rushm'quick and the foreman came out with a map, over which they pored as the launch and tender were being fuelled. Sid strained his ears to catch something of what was going on, but Rushm'quick and the foreman kept their voices low and huddled the map between them. In the end he had found out nothing fresh. The boats set off, one downstream, one up; the Old Man was still phoning all round the option, and once more the yard settled down to its busy Saturday.

It was the middle of the afternoon when Rushm'quick got back. There was more than irritation in his look now. He slammed the door of the office behind him and a moment later the window, but Sid, throwing shame to the winds, nipped round the back of the office and clapped his ear to the wooden wall. He held this pose for quite five minutes – five rapt, enthralled minutes. Then he sneaked away down to the wet boat-house, where half a dozen others were awaiting his intelligence.

'Drowned?' demanded Fidown. 'I lay my bottom dollar on a drowning.'

'Drowning – naow! You've got it on the brain.'

Sid paused for a delicious moment while the others hung on his words.

'It's the *Harrier* – burned out up by Ollby Deek.'

'Burned out?' echoed Fidown.

'Yeh – burned down flat to the water. And they found the bloke on it . . . all that's left of him. The Old Man's ringing the police up now.'

And he feasted his eyes on his mates' incredulous faces.

There was a light on in Superintendent Walker's office. Inspector Hansom knocked and went through without waiting for a reply. Inside the super, lean and keen-looking despite the hour, sat at his desk studying an interim report: he knew the way Hansom came into a room and didn't bother to look up.

'All right,' he said. 'Let's have the rest of it.'

Hansom sank his burly frame on to the visitor's chair. 'There's a helluva lot of it to tell . . .'

'Complications?' The super glanced up shrewdly.

'You can say that again. I hardly know where to begin.'

He sighed and made a pass at his cigar-pocket, but the super was a strict non-smoker, so it was only a pass. From down the corridor could be heard the clink of cups and there was an empty coffee cup at the super's elbow. Hansom eyed it pensively.

'Well, to start with, there's no doubt about the corpse. That's the one sure thing in the mess. There's some cuff-links, a signet ring that didn't quite melt and some bits of cloth that got protected in the crooks of the legs. The family have vouched for all of them. And here's the bonus for a good detective.'

Hansom fetched out a little package wrapped in a handkerchief and untied it on the super's desk. It contained a set of dentures, charred and a bit twisted in front but undamaged behind. The super stared at them unmoved.

'You've traced the dental mechanic?'

'I got his dentist's address from his wife. He identified them and double-checked with the mechanic. Lammas only had them made a few months back.'

The super nodded and pushed the relics back to Hansom.

'Tell me some more. Have you established the cause of death?'

'The pathologist is working on it, but it could be accidental. The *Harrier* is a small auxiliary yacht with the

4

engine in the well. The corpse was lying beside it and there's indications that the cover was off the engine when the fire started. But' – Hansom shrugged wearily – 'that's where the complications start.'

'Go on,' said the super.

'Well, he seems to have had a woman with him – I got that out of them at the boatyard.'

'Not his wife?'

'Definitely not his wife. His wife didn't know anything about the trip – he told her he was away on business.'

'Do we know who she was?'

'I've got a pretty sound idea. He had a secretary called Linda Brent. She hadn't been in at the office since the Saturday previous and according to her mother she left with a suitcase, saying she was going to Gayton Holiday Camp. I've checked there, but they hadn't heard of her. I got a photograph from her mother, but I haven't had time to try it on any one.'

He produced a print from his wallet. It showed a curvaceous beach-girl with straight black hair, a heart-shaped face and appealing, wide-set eyes.

'Quite a dish, isn't she . . . though mind you, his wife isn't to be sneered at.'

The super sniffed, but didn't curtail his examination of the exhibit.

'She wasn't in the wreck?'

'Nope. And she wasn't at home, either.'

'Nobody seen her?'

'Nobody we've asked yet. And that isn't all – Lammas' chauffeur is missing too. According to the servants he said Lammas rang him last night with instructions to pick him up at Ollby. He took off in the car at 8.30 p.m. and that's the last anyone's seen of him. We found the car ditched in some trees at Panxford.'

'And what time was the conflagration?'

'We've got an old fellow at Ollby village who thought he saw smoke over that way at about 9.30 p.m. It's so damned remote out there at Ollby.'

'There's a marsh-track through to the dyke, isn't there?'

'Yep. About half a mile.'

'Did you see any tyre-marks?'

'Two sets, going and coming, and the place at the end where the car turned round. They match the tyres on Lammas' car.'

The super picked irritably at the report sheet. 'Put me in the picture,' he said. 'I can't quite get it all. Give me the Lammas set-up to begin with.'

Hansom shifted in his seat and made another abortive pass at his cigar-pocket.

'All right!' snapped the super. 'Smoke, if you bloody well have to!'

Hansom acknowledged the concession gratefully. A certain peaked look left his semi-handsome features as he sucked in the first mouthful of Havana.

'James William Lammas, fifty-four, belongs to an old Norchester family . . . trades as a provision wholesaler in the city, Lammas Wholesalers Ltd., Count Street . . . wife and daughter the minor shareholders . . . wife about ten years younger . . . son, Paul, aged twenty, second year at Cambridge . . . daughter, Pauline, aged twenty-one, works at the business. In 1938 he had a big bungalow built at Wrackstead Broad. Before that he lived in the city. On Friday last he told his wife he was going to London for a week to attend a wholesalers' conference – there was one on – and briefed his head clerk to carry on the week without him. In fact he had hired the *Harrier* for a week. He turned up at the yard late on the Saturday evening when most of them had gone home, referred to the woman he'd got with him as his daughter and set off downstream. On the Friday night the *Harrier* was up Ollby Dyke. At 8.30 p.m. the chauffeur, Joseph Hicks, alleges a call from Lammas and goes off in the car. At 9.30 p.m. Jabez Tooley of "The Cot", Ollby—'

'Yes, I know all about that!' broke in the super tetchily. 'It's the family I want to hear about. What were *they* doing last night?'

Hansom puffed expensively. 'The daughter's got an alibi. The other two were just out.'

'How do you mean – just out?'

'Mrs Lammas has got her own car. She says she drove to Sea Weston.'

'Which is in the opposite direction to Ollby. And the son?'

'He was out on his motorbike.'

'And anywhere but near Ollby!'

Hansom nodded. 'Says he went as far as Cheapham.'

The super drummed on the desk with his fingers. 'I don't like it,' he said. 'I don't like it at all. And I suppose nobody knew about Lammas' fancy woman?'

'Not according to what they say.'

'Just one big surprise.'

'That's the way it's played.'

The super drummed some more and threw dirty looks at Hansom's cigar.

'All right,' he said at last. 'Let's take it in easy stages. Let's pretend everyone is telling the truth. So the chauffeur gets his call from Lammas – where did Lammas make the call?'

'There's a phone-box near where the marsh-track joins the road.'

'Right. We'll assume he used it. Now, why did Lammas want the car? Answer, to send his tootsie home so that he didn't have to sail in with her on a crowded Saturday morning.'

'Meaning his chauffeur knows about his tootsie,' put in Hansom brightly.

'Precisely,' returned the super cuttingly. 'It's something that chauffeurs usually do know about, Hansom. Now the chauffeur arrives – picks up the female – while he's there, let's say, Lammas asks him something about the yacht's engine. He gets the cover off to show him – petrol leak – makes a spark somehow – woof – chauffeur jumps clear – Lammas perishes in the flames. It's plausible, Hansom, completely plausible . . . up to that point. But now the chauffeur and the female, instead of going for help, decide to disappear. Why? What possible motive?'

'They might have been in love?' suggested Hansom.

'That's not a reason!'

'She's the sort of female a man would want to disappear with.'

'But why disappear with her *just then*?' snorted the

super. 'Surely there were other and better times? No – they must have had a stronger motive than that.'

'Like having quarrelled with Lammas and bumped him off.'

'No, man, no! If they'd done that and simply left a corpse, *that* would have been a reason. But if it was murder, it was made to look like an accident. And the only way it would keep looking like an accident would be for everyone to act naturally, which they haven't done. So we're back with the assumption that it was an accident.'

A frown crept over the Hansom brow. 'If they'd known he'd got money with him; that might have been it.'

'Money?' barked the super. 'What money had he got with him?'

Hansom stirred uneasily. 'I said it was complicated . . . he seems to have cashed out on his business.'

The super looked as though he would bite him. 'Go on,' he said dangerously. 'Take your time. Tell me when you feel like it. I'm only the Joe around here.'

'Well . . . his head clerk came across with it. Lammas had left him a cheque to draw the wages. He presented it yesterday morning and the bank told him the account was closed. And that isn't the whole story either. He'd been reducing stock during the last few months till it was practically at zero, also the lease falls through at the end of the month, also he'd closed his personal account at the bank. I made the bank give and we reckoned he had collected between seven and eight thousand pounds in small denomination notes, besides anything else he might have had. Now if he'd had that lot on board with him . . .'

'Yes, Hansom,' prompted the super witheringly. 'Don't stop . . . if he'd *had* that lot on board with him?'

'Well, it might explain why the chauffeur and the tootsie lit out . . . whether they bumped him off or whether they didn't.'

The super breathed deeply. '*Thank* you, Hansom,' he said. 'Thank you very much. And are there any other minor details you would like to mention before we try to pick up the pieces?'

Hansom indicated that there weren't and the super snorted viciously.

'Now . . . getting back to where we were. Let's just *say* he had the money with him, shall we? He had the money, and during the course of the week his female finds out about it. She tips off the chauffeur – perhaps she tries to smuggle the money off the yacht in her bag. Then one of two things happens. Either there is a genuine accident, or else Lammas finds out what is going on and they have to silence him. Now if it was an accident they might conceivably cut and run, though there would be no need for it. If it was murder arranged to look like an accident then they wouldn't run anyway, because it would defeat its own purpose. The only logical circumstance in which they would run would be if they had stolen the money and left *without knowing* about the accident – that's to say, before it happened. Isn't that so, Hansom? Doesn't it make some sort of sense out of the facts?'

Hansom wagged his cigar-stump dumbly. The super had a bad habit of making sense out of facts.

'Very well,' continued the super more agreeably. 'Let's not rush our fences. There's enough homicide going about without people vamping up cases. We'll keep an open mind, of course. The investigation will continue on its merits. But I feel pretty certain, from what you've discovered so far—'

He broke off and snatched the receiver from a ringing phone.

'Superintendent Walker . . . good . . . what did you find . . . you DID!!! Are you certain of that? . . . of course . . . send it right away.'

He slammed down the receiver and glared at it for some moments in a black silence.

'Yes,' he said finally. 'Yes! About this murder case, Hansom . . .'

'Murder?' gaped Hansom.

'I said murder!' rapped the super. 'That's the pathologist who was on the phone. He's done his autopsy and there wasn't a trace of carbon in the lungs – and you know what that means!'

'He – he was dead before the fire?'

'It does, Hansom. It means exactly that.'

They stared at each other across the superintendental desk. A look which was almost sympathetic came into the super's sharp blue eyes.

'It's up to you, Hansom,' he said kindly. 'I won't take it away from you till I get the down.'

Hansom shook his head. 'I could see it coming all along . . . it isn't news.'

'You've got to admit it's a sticky-looking prospect.'

'I wouldn't want to stand in his way . . . and we sort of owe him a case on account of the last one.'

The super nodded. 'I think it's a wise decision. The

CC would be crying out for it anyway when he gets the report . . .'

He picked up the phone again and rattled on the rest.

'Get me Central Office, CID,' he said.

Inspector Hansom laughed mirthlessly from the gloomy depths of his soul.

CHAPTER TWO

TWO FIGURES EMERGED from the sanctified dimness of the Norchester City Police HQ and paused, blinking, in the sudden stab of June sunlight. One of them was a tall, bulky, middle-aged man in a baggy tweed jacket. He carried a raincoat over his arm and wore a battered trilby on his head. The other figure, not so tall though no less bulky, was carrying a pair of suitcases which he dropped gratefully on the top step.

'And here we are again, sir,' he observed aggrievedly. 'Whisked away from the Sunday joint – and me going to take the nippers to the fair, too. I ask you, who'd be a flipping copper?'

Chief Inspector Gently smiled distantly at the empty street.

'The call of duty, Dutt. People never consider the police when they're planning a homicide.'

'I know, sir . . . but this lot here might've waited till Monday before running to the Yard. It wouldn't've hurt them to do a bit more of the donkey work.'

Gently shrugged and felt in his pocket for his pipe. He was feeling much the same himself. It was glamorous weather for a fishing expedition and he had sat up the previous evening greasing a new-pattern line he had just bought . . .

'Anyway, Dutt, it's a case that bristles with leads. We shan't be groping around for them.'

'That's one blessing, sir.'

'You might even say there's too many, from one point of view . . .'

A police Wolseley came shooting round the corner from the garage and pulled up with the merest squeal of tyres. Out of it jumped Hansom.

'We've got you some digs, though they aren't very grand . . . everything's taken out there at this time of the year.'

'They'll do,' said Gently philosophically. 'Where are they?'

'It's a bungalow at Upper Wrackstead Dyke, about a mile and a half from the village.'

'Same side as Lammas' place?'

'Good Lord no! Only the toffs live that side.'

Dutt lugged the suitcases into the car and they set off through the Sunday-still streets. It was about eight miles to Wrackstead, eight miles of gently undulating, partly wooded country, where fields of tall wheat and barley shimmered in the sun and dog-roses prinked the hedges. Hansom indicated a beech avenue leading off to the right.

'You go down there to the Lammas' place.'

'It's a good way from the village?'

'Hell, yes. Right at the end, with a frontage on the broad. There are several other places down there with river frontages, but Lammas' is the only one on the broad. I reckon he had the most money.'

'Who lives in the other places?'

'All Norchester people who've made a pile.'

'And Ollby Dyke – where would that be from here?'

'Oh, that's five or six miles downstream. The trading wherries used to use it before the road killed them. It's been neglected for years and all grown up with alder carrs – you couldn't pick a better spot for some homicide.'

They came to the river, a long reach flanked with wooden boat-sheds, irregular quays and backed by tall trees. The sun flashed off the water like liquid gold. There were crowds of limp-sailed yachts and lazy-moving motor cruisers. A humpback bridge of ancient brick and stone switchbacked them straight into the village and Gently called a halt while he investigated the possibilities of the local tobacconist.

'He's gunning for the chauffeur, is he?' jerked Hansom jealously to Dutt, in the great man's absence.

'The Chief Inspector never jumps to conclusions,' replied Dutt guardedly.

'Well, if it isn't the chauffeur, Lammas must have committed suicide . . . I can't see how the family ties in, apart from being liars.'

Gently returned with his haul of Navy Cut and they continued through the village. It was an unfortunate place, grown up round the boat-letting industry: it comprised the worst styles of the twenties and thirties in a surprising variety. But it was small — it had that to recommend it. At the railway station it was knifed off sharply and the road proceeded to Upper Wrackstead in rural purity.

Arriving there, it was met by what seemed like a cart track and the Wolseley rocked violently as it nosed down between high hedges to the river-bank below.

'Here we are,' sneered Hansom. 'The Grand Hotel of Upper Wrackstead . . . I told you you ought to stop in town.'

Gently viewed the solitary brick-and-pantile cottage without concern.

'I like to be at the centre of things if possible . . .'

'You'll be at the centre here — and how!'

But Gently was already pushing up the path to the cottage.

It was primitive, but there were compensations. One of them was the late lunch which Mrs Grey, their hostess, had been thoughtful enough to lay on. And she didn't ask questions, Gently noticed; that was a point in any landlady's favour. One might do worse than to come down here for a spot of fishing sometime.

But if Mrs Grey wasn't curious, the rest of Upper Wrackstead made up for her. There was a houseboat colony in the Dyke alongside and the arrival of a police car stirred it up like an ant-heap tickled with a stick.

'Lot of loafers!' grumbled Hansom, scowling at them through the window as he stood drinking a country-size cup of tea. 'Look as though they've never seen a policeman before!'

Gently surveyed them more mildly.

'I suppose they all come off the boats?'

'If they don't they're living in holes in the ground . . . there's nothing else at Upper Wrackstead!'

'Just at the moment, I'm rather interested in people who live here on boats.'

Interested or not, they were due to run the gauntlet. An admiring audience of nondescripts were collected about the car and as the three policemen came out they were the cynosure of at least twenty pairs of eyes.

'Coo – they've come to 'rest ole mother Grey!' exclaimed a ragged urchin, half-jeering, half-serious.

'No they ha'nt – they've come to take your mother away 'cause her old man's a burglar!' cried another.

'Johnny, you keep your trap shut!' shouted a tall slatternly woman, making a grab at him. But Johnny eluded the grab and dodged round the back of a plump, shiny-faced virago, whose face was turning an angry red.

'Here she is, mister!' he shouted to Gently. 'She's the one you're looking for' – and then, continuing in a sing-song – 'My ole man's a burglar – my ole man's a burglar – my ole man – !'

At which point a clout on the ear from the red-faced one sent him howling to his mother's skirts.

'Hold it!' exclaimed Gently, seeing that the quarrel was about to continue at a higher level. 'This isn't the way to behave on Sunday!'

'Vicious!' screamed the slattern. 'She nee'nt have give him one like that!'

'I'll give you one, much less him!' riposted the fat woman, brandishing her fist.

'And your ole man *is* a burglar!'

17

'You ha'nt *got* an ole man – kids an all!'

'Say that again!'

'I'll say it twice-times over!'

'Go on – just you dare!'

'Me dare! I dare say a few other things, too!'

'Whoa!' interposed Gently, coming suddenly between the intending combatants. 'You've got company, ladies – you just aren't supposed to carry on like this under the eyes of the law!'

There was an undecided moment while the light of battle still blazed on both sides, then the crisis passed and the slattern edged away with a muttered: 'Her ole man *is* a burglar, whatever anyone say!'

'And so he is!' cried the fat woman over Gently's shoulder. 'And s'pose he is, what's it got to do with you?'

'As long as he isn't on our current wants list . . .' murmured Gently.

The fat woman gave him a wink. 'He's doing time, don't you worry . . . they pulled him in eighteen months ago.'

'Your name Packer?' inquired Hansom from the rear.

'That's right,' said the fat woman, turning to him. '*You* should know – it was you what give the evidence at the 'sizes.'

'And were you living here then?' queried Gently.

'Me? Course I was! Spent me whole married life on the ole *Muriel* over there.' She pointed with her thumb to a dilapidated wherry lying moored, or rather stranded, in the Dyke.

'Then you know the other residents . . .?'

18

'Every last one of them.'

'You'd know, for instance, if there were any new-comers in the colony?'

'You bet I would – Pedro here come last.'

'Pedro?'

Gently turned to inspect a shrinking figure which tried to hide itself behind the other bystanders.

'Here – come on, Pedro!' exclaimed the fat woman. 'Nobody's going to hurt you. He's an Eyetie, mister, ex-prisoner of war he is. Sort of lives on the old *Muriel* with me while me old man's in the country.'

Pedro grinned sheepishly in acknowledgement. He was something over thirty, tall but rather slight, with curly dark hair and frank grey eyes.

'Don't speak a sight of English now,' added the fat woman maternally, 'but he's a good boy, all the same.'

'And when did he arrive?'

''Bout Easter. I'd say.'

'And there's been nobody since?'

'There's Ted over there – Ted Thatcher, he come here about the same time.'

'Nobody recently – yesterday, say, or late Friday night . . .?'

The fat woman paused, a gleam of intelligence dawning in her small black eyes.

'Now I'm with you, mister . . . it's Joe Hicks the shoofer you're after, i'nt it?'

'You know Hicks?' enquired Gently in surprise.

'Know him? Course I know him! I'nt it his aunt there you just been calling on?'

'You mean Mrs Grey?'

19

'Who else'd I mean?'

Gently cast an interrogative glance at Hansom, who simply shrugged and looked owlish.

'And this Joe Hicks, when did you last see him?'

She wrinkled her shiny brow. 'Wednesday was his day . . . yes, that was it. He dropped in and brought his aunt some vegetables – don't ask me where he got 'em – and afterwards we had a sing-song. Pedro here is a master-boy with a concertina.'

'And that was the last time you saw him?'

'W' yes – you don't think he'd come back here after what happened, do you?'

'He has to be somewhere . . .' Gently brooded. 'Who else was at the sing-song?'

'Just us lot and Joe.'

'Anybody who *wasn't* there?'

'Don't think so, mister . . . not apart from old Ted Thatcher, of course.' She gave Gently another of her winks and dropped her voice confidentially. 'He's got a widder, has Ted . . . he's away most of the time. Would you think it now, looking at him? What some women'll fall for!'

With an inclination of her head she indicated a paunchy, disreputable-looking figure who was hopefully daubing paint on an equally disreputable house-boat, a few yards away.

'There you are . . . some of the old'ns have got more go than the youn'uns now!'

'And he was the only one who wasn't at the sing-song?' persisted Gently.

'As far as I know.'

20

Gently made as though to stroll over to him, then paused.

'When did he come back?'

'What, Ted? Well there you've got me . . . he's a sly ole bird. He just come creeping in in that ole dinghy of his, and go creeping out again . . . I reckon you'd better ask him, mister.'

'Thanks,' said Gently, 'I will.'

There was an impatient snort from Hansom, but it was disregarded. Gently went across to the decrepit houseboat and stood admiring it as though houseboats were a grand passion in his life . . .

'Brightening it up a bit?' he inquired unhurriedly.

The painter dipped his brush and scrubbed some more paint into a weathered strake before replying.

'Ah . . .' he said indifferently.

'She hasn't had a lick lately, I'd say.'

'No more she ha'nt, bor, no more she ha'nt.'

'They tell me you were away on Wednesday,' pursued Gently, propping himself up against the cabin.

Ted Thatcher paused and turned about to look at his interrogater. He was a picturesque figure. A man in his sixties, plump, stooped a little, there was still a vitality in his bearing that promised many summers yet. He wore a shapeless brown jacket over a greasy waistcoat that wrinkled over his paunch and some sack-like trousers were stuffed into the tops of much-patched rubber boots. His face was ruddy and broad-featured. He had several days' growth of grizzled beard, but very little grey seemed to have touched his untidy hair.

21

'An' *who*,' he asked with heavy sarcasm, 'are *they*, bor, if that i'nt too much of a secret?'

'Oh . . . Mrs Packer could be the lady's name.'

'That blodda ole whure! I mighta guessed it.'

He spat contemptuously into the Dyke.

'Well . . . were you away?'

Thatcher looked at him sharply.

'Woss it got to dew wi' yew?'

'I don't know yet . . . I was wondering if you could tell me.'

There was a pause while Thatcher stirred about in a nearly-empty paint-can. Then his eyes jumped up suddenly under strangely bald brows.

'Yew'r a blodda ole copper, aren't yew, bor?' he asked gruffly.

Gently grinned. 'I blodda am, tew . . .'

'Blast!' exclaimed Thatcher in amazement. 'Yew aren't agorn to tell me yew come from these parts?'

'I don't, but I've been around them quite a bit.'

Thatcher's broad features relaxed a little and then he grinned too.

'Verra well, my man . . . dew yew think tha's gorna help yew. I've been away above a week, an' come back Frida. Woss the nex' question?'

'Have you been very far?'

'Jus' a little trip in my dingha.'

'Would it be indiscrete to ask where?'

'That would,' retorted Thatcher stoutly. 'So yew might as well not ask m'.'

'Let's put it another way. Was where you were coming from the other side of Ollby Dyke?'

22

'W'in a general sorta way, yes, it was.'

'And you passed Ollby Dyke on the Friday?'

'I woon't ha' got here dew I ha'nt.'

'About what time did you pass it?'

'Oh, I dunno ... six or seven o'clock time, woon't s'prise me.'

'You couldn't make it about nine, could you?' broke in Hansom sardonically from behind.

'No, I blodda couldn't – not for yew nor a dozen like yew!'

'Were there,' continued Gently patiently, 'many boats about when you went by?'

'W' yes ... tha's pretta busy this time of year.'

'Do you remember any of them?'

'Can't say I dew.'

'Were there any in Ollby Dyke?'

'Not enna yew could see – tha's tew growed-up.'

'You didn't see Mr Lammas, for instance.'

'Woon't know him if I did.'

'He was on the yacht *Harrier* as you probably know.'

'Nor I di'nt see that neether, so there yew are, ole partna.'

Gently sighed, and felt in his pocket for a peppermint cream. He was obviously pushing his luck too hard at Upper Wrackstead.

'And what did it buy you?' jeered Hansom, as they got back into the Wolseley.

'*Tingere barbam non potes*,' murmured Gently oracularly.

'Eh?' gaped Hansom.

'Never mind – it's a classical tag I picked up somewhere. We'll leave Mr Thatcher with one of his secrets, shall we?'

CHAPTER THREE

S LOLEY'S BOATYARD LAY at the end of a long,
low cinder-track, a track which was crowded at each
side with yards and bungalows. It consisted of several dry
and wet boat-sheds clustered round a cut-in from the river
and, on a Sunday afternoon, was deserted by both boats and
men. The office was open, however, and Old Man Sloley
sat at his desk, a silent figure in frock-coat and peaked cap,
his white beard straggling down on the blotter in front of
him. He rose stiffly as the three policemen entered.

'Good afternoon, gentlemen . . . I was expecting a
call from you. Have you made any progress in this
shocking business yet?'

He indicated one of the more lurid Sunday papers,
which was lying on his desk. 'BODY IN BROADS
BURN-OUT' was the punch-line on page one.

Hansom introduced Gently and the old man shook
hands. There was an unexpected fragility about him, as
though a gust of wind would have blown him away.

'Mr Sloley is ninety-two . . .' murmured Hansom in
an aside.

Old Man Sloley nodded, as though to warn them of his perfect hearing.

'This has been a grave shock to me, gentlemen, a very grave shock. This firm has never had a breath of scandal attached to its name before.'

Gently assured him that no blame could be placed to the account of Sloley & Son, but Old Man Sloley would not be convinced.

'It's kind of you, Mr Inspector, but you haven't read the papers; there are cruel insinuations being made. And I assure you, that except for my son I would have refused this let. I was not imposed upon by the gentleman describing the young lady as his daughter.'

'You knew it was not Miss Lammas, sir?'

'No, Mr Inspector, I have not the pleasure of Miss Lammas' acquaintance. Neither did I know Lammas personally . . . the people over the river come mostly from Norchester, you know, they are very rarely seen in the village. But it seemed most peculiar to me that these two people should hire what was veritably a single-cabined yacht, and when I saw them I had the strongest misgivings.'

'When did the actual hiring take place, sir?' asked Gently.

'On the twenty-third of March,' replied Old Man Sloley, with unpausing precision.

'In March! Is it usual to book so early?'

'That is not early, Mr Inspector, it is late. We are usually fully booked by that date.'

'Was it a personal application?'

'No sir, it was not. Mr Lammas rang this office and

inquired what we could offer him for the week in question. As it happened I had a cancellation for the *Harrier* and he agreed to take it. When I understood that his daughter would accompany him I pointed out that complete privacy could not be had on such a small boat, but he brushed the objection aside. The booking was confirmed by a letter from his business address and a cheque for the deposit.'

'You will have that letter, sir . . .?'

The old man opened a drawer and took out a manilla envelope.

'I had it ready, Mr Inspector . . . I felt it might be helpful to you. Here is also our copy of the booking form, together with a plan of the *Harrier* and some photographs of her. Please tell me if you need anything else.'

'Thank you, sir. It isn't often we get such thoughtful co-operation.' Gently tucked the envelope away in his breast pocket. 'I'd like to know the approximate time at which the yacht was taken over.'

'Yes, sir. It was at 9 p.m.'

'You were in the office?'

'No, it was my son who received Mr Lammas. But I saw them shortly afterwards, when they came down to the yacht.'

'And you suspected there was no relationship between Mr Lammas and his companion?'

'I did, Mr Inspector. There was not a scrap of resemblance between them.'

'Could you describe the lady?'

'I could, sir. She was above the middle height, a little obvious in her figure and had black, straight hair, worn somewhat longer than is usual in these days. Her complexion was pale and she had a delicate chin. She spoke quickly in what I may call a rather high-pitched voice.'

Gently nodded to Hansom, who produced his photograph. 'Would this be her, sir . . .?'

The old man took it in his knotty hand and examined it attentively.

'Yes, sir, I think it would. But you must understand she was dressed with greater propriety when I saw her.'

'Well, that's settled the identity problem,' observed Hansom as they went down to the quay, where Rushm'quick awaited them in the yard-launch.

'Rattled it off like a portrait-parley, he did,' put in Dutt admiringly. 'Who'd've thought the old gent had a memory like that?'

'But why did she go off with the chauffeur?' mused Gently from the back of beyond.

'Why did she go off with him?' echoed Hansom.

'Yes — she didn't have to, did she? Lammas himself was obviously planning to skip with her.'

'They might have quarrelled, or she might have preferred a younger man . . .'

Gently shook his head in the irritating way he had.

Rushm'quick cast off and turned the launch downstream. The river was flocking with pleasure-craft of every kind, drifting yachts, busy motor-cruisers, skiffs, launches and majestic trip-boats. On the south bank were the bungalows. Timber-and-plaster surmounted by deep reed thatch, they nestled under downy willows and behind great velvet lawns. No Moorings, said the little white noticeboards at their quay-heads, No Moorings, No Moorings. There were no moorings anywhere on that bank.

A mile further down the last bungalow hedged off its lawns from the wilderness, and a tangle of impenetrable alder and willow carr succeeded.

'Lammas' place is the other side of that lot,' remarked Hansom, by way of commentary. 'Do you want to see them today?'

'Not today . . . we'll let them have Sunday in peace.'

Hansom snorted at such an unpoliceman-like sentiment.

They saw the bungalow, however, when they turned into the broad. It stood far back at the top end, looking tiny and lost in the surrounding carrs and reed-islands. Like most of the outlying bungalows it was high-built on black-painted timber piles, the space beneath being utilized as a wet boat-house.

'Are there any boats in there?' asked Gently.

'There's a launch and a half-decker – maybe a couple of dinghies.'

'Lammas do much sailing?'

Hansom extended his two hands. 'I didn't get round to his hobbies.'

They throbbed away down the broad and out into the river again.

Now it was continuous, the wilderness, breaking only to disclose reed-choked waterways. Once they passed a headland of firm ground falling down to a little sand beach, but the rest was all carr or shaking reedways. But there was nothing lonely about it. Not on a fine Sunday

28

at the end of June. Rushm'quick, with three policemen on board, had a tense time of it sticking strictly to the rules in the handbook.

'Here we are,' he jerked at last with relief. 'That's the entrance to Ollby Dyke . . . down there at the end of the reach.'

It was necessary to point it out. The inexpert eye would have seen nothing just there except tangled carr and ferocious brambles. But an inlet there was, using a bit of force-work, and on the far side one caught a glimpse of a narrow dyke disappearing into the fastness of the carrs.

'He must have known the country pretty well . . .' brooded Gently. 'How did he get a yacht up there?'

'It'd go in all right if he had the mast down.'

'There's a keel on a yacht.'

'Ah, but there's a spring up Ollby Dyke . . . that keeps plenty of water in it. Shall I take her in?'

'No – wait just a moment.'

A couple of hundred yards further down on the other bank the carrs fell away and there, just visible among the bushes, was an old houseboat pulled out. And there was a ribbon of grey smoke rising above it.

'Someone live there?'

'Only old Noggins, the eel-catcher.'

'Let's go and see him first . . . we should have something in common.'

Obediently Rushm'quick spun his wheel and sent the launch weaving downstream again.

The eel-catcher sat on an eel-chest in front of his make-shift lodging. He was a little man of indeterminable age, dressed in a drab jacket and trousers out of which the rest of him seemed to grow, as though it were all part of him. He eyed the launch unfavourably as it pulled in alongside.

'Yew be careful where yew're comin – I got a pair of eel-trunks down there!'

'Think I didn't know that?' growled Rushm'quick.

'Well I'm tellin on yew – jus to make sure!'

He got up reluctantly and came over to them. Gently introduced himself briefly.

'You didn't happen to be here Friday evening, I suppose?'

'Frida evening – w'yes! I had m'nets up Frida.'

'You were here all the evening?'

'Ah, most of the day asides.'

'And do you remember seeing Sloley's *Harrier* go by?'

'Thatta dew, and saw the bloke what was on it tew.'

'Tell me,' said Gently simply.

The little man's face puckered up. 'W' . . . that was about eight o'clock time, I reckon. There'd been all sorts goin past – I shoonta noticed in the ordinara way. But this bloke fetches up on the bank here to pull his mast down . . . naturalla, I keep an eye on him.'

'And then?'

'W' then he start his ingin and slide off again, an the last I see of him was goin up the Deek.'

Gently hesitated. 'Did you know who he was?'

'Blast no! Woont know him from Adam.'

'Or the woman with him?'

'He ha'nt got no woman.'

'What was that?'

30

'I say he ha'nt got no woman. That was jus him on his lonesome.'

There was a moment broken only by the throb of the idling motor and then Hansom exploded angrily:

'Of *course* he had a bloody woman – we know all about it!'

'I tell yew he *ha'nt*,' retorted the little man obstinately.

'You mean you didn't see her – she was in the cabin.'

'No she wa'nt. He was moored starn-on, an I could see down into the cabin. Sides, why di'nt she help him get the mast down? That wa'nt easa for him, on his own.'

'She could have been in the WC!' snarled Hansom.

'Then she musta been wholla bound up, tha's all I can say . . .'

He wasn't to be shaken – there was only Lammas on the *Harrier* that evening. Neither Hansom's bullying nor Gently's more subtle methods would make him modify his statement.

'What was he wearing?' queried Gently at the end of it.

'W'one of them sports shuts an some white trousers.'

'You're sure it was a sports shirt?'

'I aren't blind, ama? That was a red one.'

'A tall, heavily built man, was he?'

'No, that he wa'nt, jus midlin' an a bit on the lean side.'

Gently nodded absently and signed to Rushm'quick to push off.

'We may be back for another chat later on, Mr Noggins.'

'The old fool's got his lines mixed!' grunted Hansom as they chugged back towards the Dyke. 'The woman was out of sight and he'll swear blind she wasn't there.'

'What about his description of Lammas?'

'That tallies all right . . . the bits of trouser we recovered were white flannel.'

'And his build?'

'Like he said – medium height and spare.'

'Which leaves the sports shirt, doesn't it . . .?'

'Sports shirt?' Hansom stared.

'Yes . . . didn't you find the cuff-links with the body? It looks as though Lammas changed his shirt.'

'Christ yes – he must have done!' The divine light of ratiocination appeared in Hansom's eye. 'Yeh – there might be something in Noggins's story at that. Suppose he put the female off somewhere down-river – he brings the yacht up here to hide it and kill the trail for a day or two – changes into his city clothes and rings his chauffeur, the chauffeur being paid to keep his mouth shut—'

'You're forgetting one thing, though . . .'

'What's that?'

'He'd got his trail covered for the whole week. He might just as well have lit out on the previous Saturday, saying nothing to nobody.'

Hansom sniffed in a deprived sort of way. 'We've got to make sense of the facts, haven't we?'

They ducked as Rushm'quick sent the launch slicing through the drooping boughs and bushes that concealed the mouth of the Dyke. On the other side they seemed to be in a different world. Overhead the tangled twigs of blunt-leaved alder closed out the sky, on either hand the stretching rubbish reached out to brush the launch as it slid past. A green-lit tunnel it was, thrusting remotely into a forgotten land.

Hansom snatched a dead alder burr out of his hair.

'Thirty years ago there were wherries up and down here every day of the year.'

It was only half a mile long, but there seemed no end to it. One hemmed-in reach followed another with bewildering monotony. And then, just as Gently's sense of direction was irretrievably lost, the alders parted overhead and they swung out into blazing afternoon sunlight.

They were in a little pool, grown up and almost choked with reeds, water-lilies and a myriad-flowered water-plant. On the far side, against the rotted remnants of a quay, lay the fire-blasted yacht. And by the yacht sat a Police Constable smoking a cigarette, his tunic and helmet hung on a willow-snag.

'Jackson!' bawled Hansom, in a voice to wake the dead.

The Constable jumped as though he had been stung.

'What the blue blazes do you think you're supposed to be doing – having the day off?'

'I – I wasn't really expecting anyone . . .!' blurted the Constable, struggling into his tunic.

'Oh, you weren't, eh?' commented Hansom nastily. 'Thought we'd come by car and you'd hear us in time, didn't you . . .?'

Rushm'quick eased the bows of the launch against the rotten quay and they jumped down gingerly on to shaky green turf. The yacht lay well in under the trees, which bore silent witness to the fierceness of the blaze. It was completely gutted. From end to end the interior showed a blackened mass of ash, nothing remaining of cabin, deck or fitments. Only the engine jutted up near the stern and the charred ribs preserved a pathetic symmetry.

Gently sniffed at the acrid smell of burned varnish.

'Was the body this side of the engine or the other?'

'The other.'

'Was the petrol-tank that side?'

'Yes – you can see where it blew out.'

'There must have been a lot of petrol used to do a job like this . . . is it safe to go aboard?'

He stepped cautiously on to the hulk and was directly up to his ankles in ashes, which still seemed warm. He kicked them away from the engine and stooped to examine it.

'Did you find the carburettor?'

'No, it was too bloody hot to look for carburettors the last time I was here!'

Gently poked about in the ash with his foot and was eventually rewarded.

'Looks as though it was unscrewed. The cap's off it, too.'

'Reckon he took the cap off first,' put in Rushm'quick knowingly, 'then it wasn't coming through fast enough, so he took the carb right off.'

Gently nodded and continued to probe with his foot. Towards the fore part of the hulk his shoe caught something which sounded hollow and metallic. The twisted remains of a jerrican came to light.

'Is this part of the yacht's equipment?'

Rushm'quick shook his head.

Gently handed it out and clambered back on to the bank.

'Well ... there's a nasty job for someone, going through those ashes. We'd better have it towed back to the yard and gone over there. How do you get a car into an outpost like this?'

Hansom led the way along a doubtful track which plunged through the thick of the surrounding wilderness. But a few yards saw them on higher, drier ground and the track widened into a lane.

'Here you are – you can still see the tracks where he turned the car.'

'Where does the lane go?'

'It joins the Lockford–Wrackstead road about a mile from Ollby. The phone-box is at the junction.'

'No houses about there?'

'There's a bloke called Marsh lives in a house a quarter of a mile towards Panxford, but the house stands back amongst trees. He didn't see anything ... *no* bastard's seen anything! All we've got is the village idiot.'

Gently tutted. 'You can't manufacture witnesses. Have you searched the area round here?'

'We didn't get time to be really clever.'

'Then you mightn't have noticed ... *that* ... for instance?'

He pointed to the bole of an alder a few yards off the track. A white flake was showing up against the dark, gnarled bark.

35

Hansom glared at it as though it were a personal insult. 'And what's that supposed to be – the answer to a detective's prayer?'

But Dutt had already grasped the significance of the white flake and was making his way carefully through the rough grass. Gently waited patiently, Hansom impatiently, while the sergeant performed his operation. Eventually there was a little cluck of triumph from Dutt and he returned to drop something small in his superior's hand. Gently examined it expressionlessly.

'Spot any blood, Dutt?'

'Yessir.'

'Much or little?'

'Not much, sir.'

'Head, I expect. They'd have noticed it lower down.'

'What I was thinking, sir . . . about the angle, too.'

'Would it be too much,' enquired Hansom with biting sarcasm, 'would it be too much to ask what all this is about?'

Gently extended his hand gravely and revealed the shapeless chunk of metal Dutt had dug from the tree.

'It's about the way Lammas was killed . . . you can let your pathologist off duty. He was shot through the head with a bullet from a .22 gun.'

CHAPTER FOUR

IT WAS A pleasant run from the village to 'Willow Street', lately the home of James William Lammas. After traversing the beech avenue, the road ran along the edge of the upland just where it fell into the shallow river valley and one caught glimpses of the winding stream low down amongst billowy trees and later of the broad.

'All this and the best coarse-fishing too . . .' murmured Gently at the wheel of the Wolseley. At breakfast that morning he had watched Thatcher fairly scooping bream out of the mouth of the Dyke.

'You know, it's rum, sir,' began Dutt beside him, and stopped.

'What's rum, Dutt?'

'Well sir, it stuck in me loaf what you said about the woman.'

'What was that?'

'About her not having to go off with the shover.'

'It's a point that needs elucidating.'

'I mean, sir, it's pretty obvious that this geezer and her were planning to fade together . . . it don't seem natural

37

for her to get the shover to do him in. What's she going to get out of it what she didn't have in the first place?'

'Only the chauffeur . . . he might be quite a guy.'

'No sir.' Dutt shook his head. 'If she'd been took with the shover there wasn't nothink in their way . . . *he* wasn't married. And she wouldn't be carrying on with Lammas.'

'Unless it was a deep, dark plot.'

'No sir. It don't seem right.'

'What's the theory, then, Dutt?'

'Well, sir . . . I'd say the shover did for both of them and hooked it on his own. It's the only way what makes sense, the way I looks at it. He knows about the money – it's got to be on the boat – he goes there ready to do for them and make it look like an accident. When he gets there he finds there's only Lammas, but if he shoots him first-off down by the car he isn't going to know that till it's too late.'

'And then, Dutt?'

'And then he goes through wiv it, sir – what else can he do? But somehow he runs across the woman again – maybe Lammas was aiming to pick her up somewhere close – she's seen the fire – she sees the shover coming away from it – so he has to do for her, to keep her mouth shut. And then he dusn't go back and shove her in the yacht, so he gets rid of the corpse somewhere else.'

'Which is why he flitted, eh, Dutt? The second corpse wasn't looking like an accident.'

'That's right, sir. Otherwise he'd be sitting tight and knowing nothink.'

38

Gently grinned feebly at his subordinate. 'It's a nice little theory . . . all it needs to set it up is a bunch of facts and a fresh corpse.'

'Well, sir . . . it isn't to say they won't turn up.'

'No, Dutt – but until they do we'd better be good policemen and keep a wide-open mind.'

'Yessir. Of course, sir.'

'We're only halfway into the picture . . . it's the other half we may be finding now.'

They had come to the ornate iron gates of 'Willow Street'. The narrow country road turned sharply to the right, the gates being set in the corner. Beyond them a gravel drive screwed steeply down between luxuriant rhododendrons, now in full bloom, their giant salmon, white and heliotrope flowers seeming to explode against the sombre leaves.

'Willow Street' from the landward side presented a different picture to 'Willow Street' seen from the broad. It was not entirely a high-built bungalow. The land at this point dropped down to the carrs in a knoll, so that while the front of the building was piled the rest of it was niched into the slope, and the floor was at ground level where the drive came sweeping out of the rhododendrons. It was built in the traditional timber and white plaster, its reed thatch humping over semi-circular loft-windows. A golden vane surmounted the high cone of thatch rising at the broad end.

Hansom had already arrived from Norchester. His car stood parked near the capacious garage and he was to be seen chatting to a tiny dark woman who scarcely came up to his elbow. A Constable stood at a little distance. Gently parked and went over to them.

'Chief Inspector Gently, ma'am, in charge of the case . . . this is Mrs Lammas.'

Gently extended his hand.

She was a woman of forty or a little more, but so delicately beautiful that her age seemed to adorn rather than detract from her. Slight in build, her features were pale and small, like those of a Dresden figure, her brown eyes appearing by contrast large and curiously penetrating. She wore a plain black dress too simple to be cheap and on her finger a ring of diamonds and emeralds. Her voice, when she spoke, was low but ringingly clear.

'I am pleased to meet you, inspector . . . Inspector Hansom has just been telling me about you.'

'We are sorry to have to intrude upon you, ma'am, at a time like this.'

'It cannot be otherwise, inspector . . . I do not wish it otherwise. Will you come into the house?'

They followed her up the steps and down a wide, parquet corridor.

'This is the lounge. I trust it will suit your purpose?'

It was a large room overlooking the broad, with French windows giving on to a veranda. Gently cast a speculative eye around the furnishings. Expensive, also feminine. There was nothing in that room to suggest a man had ever lived there.

'You have a beautiful home, ma'am.'

'Thank you, inspector.'

'Your husband must have been in a substantial way of business.'

'My husband—' she began and then checked herself,

her small lips pressing tight. 'This is my own house. I built it and furnished it myself.'

'It does your taste credit.'

She rang the bell and ordered coffee to be brought. Hansom arranged his short-hand Constable at a card-table and made other official dispositions. Mrs Lammas watched him coldly.

'I suppose you will begin with me?'

Gently shrugged. 'Would it upset the domestic economy if we started with the servants?'

'Not really. Do you want the cook or the maid?'

'We'll take the maid . . . she'll be along with the coffee.'

'What do you think of her?' inquired Hansom leeringly when Mrs Lammas had retired. 'Can you imagine a man turning up a dish like that for his secretary!'

'It's surprising what men do.'

'And money with it — Lammas must have been crackers!'

'I daresay he has his point of view if you could get round to it.'

The maid came in, bearing the coffee on a silver tray. She was a square-boned, moon-faced girl in her twenties. When the coffee was served Gently bade her be seated and took his place with Hansom at the table opposite.

'Your name, please?'

'Gwyneth Jones, it is.'

'You don't belong to these parts?'

'Oh no! I come from Wales, like Mrs Lammas.'

'Mrs Lammas is Welsh?'

'Indeed she is – and good Welsh too, at that!'

Gently nodded and dropped lumps of sugar into his fragile coffee cup.

'Now Miss Jones . . . we'd like you to tell us exactly what happened on Friday evening from, shall we say, tea-time.'

'But I've told it already, I have—'

'We'd like to hear it again, if you please.'

The maid gave herself a little shake and then began, as though it were a lesson: 'The cook and me were sitting in the kitchen, we were, talking about old times at Pwllheli—'

'Whoa!' interrupted Gently. 'What time was this?'

'Oh, about eight o'clock, or it might be later.'

'But I want you to tell what happened before that.'

'There wasn't nothing happened – it just went on as it always does go on!'

'Never mind – I'd still like to hear about it.'

The maid gave herself another little shake. 'Well, there was Miss Pauline had her tea early to catch a bus—'

'How early?'

'At half-past five it was, she was catching the quarter-past six.'

'Does she usually travel by bus?'

'Oh yess! She's wonderfully independent is Miss Pauline – not like Mr Paul in that respect, mark you. In the mornings she would go to the office with her father, but when it came to her own affairs it was different.'

'She was going to a rehearsal in Norchester, I believe.'

'Indeed – she has always been a one for acting.'

'Did she usually have tea early when she was going to a rehearsal?'

'– No, not that I know of. It was the ten-to-seven bus as a rule.'

'Very well . . . go on with what you were telling me.'

'Why, then the mistress and Mr Paul has tea here, in the lounge, and very quiet they were – not the usual chatter at all. And while we were washing the dishes I heard Mr Paul starting up his motorcycle – "Look you," says I to Gwladys, "there has been a row, or something very much like one"—'

'What time was that?'

'Oh, about seven o'clock I'd say, either more or less. "If there has been a row," says Gwladys—'

'Did you actually see Mr Paul leave?'

'Oh yess, I did – the kitchen looks out that way.'

'And Mrs Lammas what time did she leave?'

'Some minutes later I was going to *tell* you!'

Gently sighed and resigned himself to be told.

'"If there has been a row," says Gwladys, "a quiet one it has been, I tell you," and while we were talking about it, out comes the mistress and has a word with Joseph. Then Joseph gets her car out, and off she goes, and it was after that he comes into the kitchen.'

'And he was in the kitchen until he was called out?'

'Yess – all the time. He often came to sit there. But mark you, as a rule he liked to gossip, and Friday night he hardly said a word. And then the phone rang. "It's like for me," he said, and goes to get it.'

'He was expecting the call?'

'I would have said so.'

43

'The telephone is in the corridor, Miss Jones. Is the kitchen near there?'

'Indeed, it's right beside it.'

'Then you were in a position to hear the conversation?'

'Oh yess – every word.'

'Can you remember anything of it?'

'I can, though not exactly. He was asking how to get to where it was.'

'And anything else?'

'No – nothing I remember.'

'You wouldn't have been close enough to have heard the voice of the person at the other end?'

She shook her head.

'Or whether it was, in fact, Mr Lammas?'

'No, I would not.'

'But that was your general impression?'

'Indeed yess, he sounded just as though he were speaking to Mr Lammas.'

'Thank you, Miss Jones ... please continue your account.'

The maid stroked down her lace-edged apron and paused before going on. There wasn't any nervousness about her, Gently noticed; the authority of the mistress descended to the servant.

'Well, Joseph hung up and told us he had to go to Ollby to fetch Mr Lammas. – "You'll miss 'Take It From Here'," says Gwladys, looking at the clock, "it's just on half-past eight, mun, why not go a little later? You can always say you've had some trouble with the car." But he would not stay, not even for a cup of tea.'

'He mentioned Mr Lammas, did he?'

44

'Oh yess, he did.'

'Go on.'

'Why, then he goes, and me and Gwladys has our tea and toast, and listen to the wireless, we do, until it's getting quite late. At last we hear Mr Paul come back on his motorcycle. He hasn't been back five minutes when the mistress follows him and when they get together in the lounge there are words, I can tell you, though they keep their voices low.'

'About what?' inquired Gently eagerly.

'I didn't hear — and if I did, I might not tell you.'

'This isn't idle curiosity, you know . . .'

'I know it isn't — but then, I didn't hear.'

Gently shrugged regretfully and motioned her to proceed.

'An hour it goes on, if not longer. I never heard the like before between them. And then Miss Pauline comes in off the bus, and look you, it's all over, just like that. The mistress rings for malted milk and biscuits, and then to bed without another word.'

'What time would that be?'

'Oh, half-past eleven at the soonest.'

'The bus gets in when?'

'Eleven o'clock, it does.'

'Hmn.'

Gently leaned back in his chair and seemed to be studying the white sails which turned and drifted on the broad below.

'Miss Jones . . . have you been very long with the Lammas family?'

'I have been here four years and three months, come Michaelmas.'

'Would you say it was a . . . happy family?'

'I daresay there are worse, when you look about you.'

'And what would you mean by that?'

She hesitated and then drew herself up with a flash of agression. 'I mean she was too good for him by far – that's what I mean! And if you're asking me, I'd say that nobody will shed many tears now he's gone!'

Gently nodded his mandarin nod.

'That's all, Miss Jones . . . will you send in the cook as you go through, please?'

Gently had tapped a source of peppermint creams in Wrackstead and he produced his bag now and offered it to Hansom. Hansom took one suspiciously to sample.

'I never could see what was so damned special about these things!'

Gently tossed one to Dutt and another to the short-hand Constable. 'They soothe the nerves, you know, and keep the brain clear.'

'There must be something in it – you seem to get results on them!'

'Try one the next time things are getting sticky . . .'

Hansom munched noisily a few moments and then said: 'What was all that about the voice on the phone?'

Gently hoisted a non-committal shoulder. 'I just like to know the minor details.'

'You got an idea it was someone else – like the secretary?'

'I keep ideas at a distance this early in a case.'

Hansom grunted and kept working on the peppermint cream.

46

'Then there's that row with the son . . . maybe that ties in somewhere. Yeah – and the way they went out and came back! It looks as though Paul's ma was trailing him, and she must have known where he was going to keep five minutes behind.'

'Could have known what the shover was up to, sir,' put in Dutt brightly. 'Might have been the son what finds out where Lammas is and gives the tinkle.'

'Yeah – and it's the *son* who's sweet on the secretary; how about that for a hunch?'

Gently held up a restraining hand. 'And you ask me what's special about peppermint creams . . .! But getting off theory for a moment, what do you see in the garden, Dutt?'

Dutt cast his intelligent eye downwards.

'Well sir, there's a bloke tying up some sweet-peas.'

'Just so, Dutt . . . we'll assume he's the gardener. Go down and have a chat with him, will you?'

'Yessir. Directly, sir.'

'Especially touching the incidence of jerricans in the garage . . .'

'I get you, sir.'

'And what other things your police-training suggests.'

Dutt clicked his heels smartly and descended to the garden by the veranda steps. At the same moment there was a confident knock at the door and the cook entered.

The cook was a dumpy middle-aged Welshwoman with a comfortable face and lively grey eyes. She came in with an expression of anticipation on her countenance, as though an incursion of policemen was something that brightened up her day, and took her seat before being asked.

'Your name, please?'

'Gwladys Roberts, spinster, look you.'

'You are Mrs Lammas' cook, I believe?'

'I am too, but my father was in the Force and my brother is a sergeant at Cwmchynledd.'

'Indeed? Then you will be familiar with the routine of interrogation, Miss Roberts . . .?'

'Why should I not, when I was brought up at a Station?'

Gently took her over the same ground as had been already covered with the maid. Her answers were full and to the point, and confirmed what they had heard before. She could add nothing to the maid's account of the conversation on the phone.

'And you have been long with the family, Miss Roberts?'

'Long, you say! They've never been without me.'

'Mrs Lammas engaged you when she got married?'

'Yess, and the first time. She's been married twice, though through no fault of hers.'

'Would you explain . . .?'

'Why, first she married Geoffrey Owen of Bangor. A gentleman he was, come of good family, and a Major in the Guards. But he didn't last long, poor fellow. He went to Aden and died there of cholera. Poor Mrs Phyllis! I thought she would have followed him . . . so bad she took it.'

'And after that she married Lammas?'

'Yess, after that.' The cook's face had become melancholy. 'We went to Torquay – Mrs Phyllis was

48

poorly. She met him at Torquay, right on the rebound, and in a week they'd done it.'

'It wasn't too . . . successful?'

'No, mun, it wasn't. Though mark you, Mr Lammas wasn't all to blame. He did his best at first to make it go. But there, they wasn't suited, that's the answer. She couldn't forget poor Mr Geoffrey and he didn't like having Mr Geoffrey thrown up at him at every turn. Ah me! It was a bad day when we went to Torquay.'

'The children . . . they didn't improve matters?'

'No, not a bit. When Mr Paul came he was all his mother's, and so he still is. Miss Pauline was her father's.'

'Would you say there was animosity between father and son?'

'Oh yess! They had some quarrels, I can tell you.'

'About anything in particular?'

'No, not at first. Mr Paul was just obstreperous and above himself – his head is full of poetry and nonsense. He used to say his proper name was Owen.'

'Would that have been possible?'

'Not on your life! He knew it wasn't, too.'

'What else did they quarrel about?'

'Oh, Mr Lammas wanted his son in the business, that was the big trouble. And Mr Paul, he wouldn't hear about it. If you ask me, Mr Paul doesn't think much of the university either, but then he only went there to spite his father.'

'That would be somewhere about two years ago?'

'Indeed it was. You never heard such rows!'

'And of course, it worsened the relationship between Mr Lammas and his wife?'

'Oh yess, she took her son's part, all the way. Some bitter things were said. It was Mrs Phyllis who sent Mr Paul to Cambridge and pays his fees. I don't think Mr Lammas ever properly got over what happened two years ago.'

Gently paused to criss-cross some lines on his scribbling pad before his next question.

'You will have heard by now, Miss Roberts, that Mr Lammas was enjoying certain relations with Miss Brent, his secretary. Was there any suspicion of this before the present juncture?'

The cook gave a little giggle. 'Oh no, I shouldn't think so. Though Miss Pauline works at the office with him – I wouldn't put it past her to know what was going on.'

'But you don't think it was suspected by Mrs Lammas?'

'Well there, I couldn't say. But if she suspected, she didn't know or there would have been more made of it.'

'Mr Lammas gave an excuse of business for his absence last week. Had he done so before?'

'Once or twice he had lately, but only for a day or so.'

'What do you mean by "lately"?'

'Why . . . he didn't use to go off much. It was only these last two or three months.'

'And Mrs Lammas accepted the excuse without comment?'

'If she didn't, I never heard about it.'

'Can you remember if these absences occurred at the weekend, or was it during the week?'

'He was always here at the weekend.'

50

Gently nodded. 'And now, Miss Roberts, we should like to hear what you can tell us about the chauffeur, Hicks . . .'

The cook folded her plump arms and cogitated a moment, as though passing the subject under review. Then she frowned and said:

'Well, you know . . . he's not the person I should have thought of to go and do a thing like that . . .'

Gently clicked his tongue. 'Perhaps you could tell us a little more?'

'Oh yess! I was just saying! But really it came as a surprise when I heard about it. I've known Joe to lose his temper, and once for certain Mr Lammas would have sacked him if Mrs Phyllis had permitted. But there wasn't no spirit in the man, he didn't have the go in him to up and kill somebody.'

'He was also a servant of long standing?'

'Indeed he was. Mrs Phyllis engaged him when she was having Mr Paul and apart from the war, when we got along without a chauffeur, he has been with us ever since. Very attached he has always been to Mrs Phyllis, besides being one of the few people Mr Paul hits it off with. Taught him to drive, he did, and likewise to fish. You could hardly drop on a man less likely to stick his neck out.'

'Taught him to fish, did he?' A dreamy expression stole into Gently's eyes and once more they wandered to the bright-lit expanse of broad with its thousand reedy inlets. He pulled himself up.

'You couldn't find a picture of him for Inspector Hansom . . . have you been able to find one since?'

'There now – I was forgetting!'

She felt in her wide apron-pocket and produced a postcard print of the sort vended by street photographers. It was taken on a promenade and showed a man of medium build in dark uniform, the maid on one arm and the cook on the other. He had a stolid but far from naive Northshire countenance. His lips were thin and his mouth rather wide.

'Took last year it was, on the front at Starmouth.'

'He looks quite presentable. Did he have any girl-friends?'

'Well, we had our larks, but I never heard of him going steady with a girl.'

'Did he ever mention Miss Brent?'

'No, not to me.'

'Had he any people or special friends in the locality?'

'Only his aunt, who lives at Upper Wrackstead.'

Gently stowed the photograph away in his wallet. 'Now we're on the subject of photographs, I don't see any of Mr Lammas about.'

The cook cast a quick look towards a bureau at the far end of the room, her eyes rounding in perplexity.

'That's funny now . . . there used to be one here. Perhaps he took it with him.'

'Are there any others?'

'Oh yess, no doubt, in Mrs Phyllis' albums.'

'But none about the house?'

'No, certainly. She would not have them there.'

'Just one more question, Miss Roberts, and then I think we can let you go.'

The cook looked up attentively.

'Was Hicks a musical man . . . did he, for instance, play a concertina?'

'Why yes he did – but very badly, though!'

'Thank you, Miss Roberts . . . that's everything for the moment.'

Hansom watched her thoughtfully as she got up and departed. Then he reached out absently towards the bag of peppermint creams. 'You're right . . .' he said to Gently, beginning to munch.

Gently cocked an interrogative eyebrow.

'About Lammas having a point of view. Me, I think I'd have cashed out in twenty months, let alone twenty years!'

CHAPTER FIVE

THERE WERE ASHTRAYS about the lounge and as though by tacit consent they all began to smoke. Hansom began it with one of his workaday Dutch whiffs, then Gently produced his weathered sand-blast. Finally the Constable, after many vain attempts to catch someone's eye, slipped out a small, thin cigarette-case, thus proving beyond doubt that Constables do carry such things about their person.

'Cancer, my arse!' observed Hansom crudely. 'Why pick on tobacco out of all the other things?'

Gently blew a comfortable ring. 'We've been smoking the stuff several centuries now . . .'

'I can show you a dozen old boys over ninety — smoked and chewed it since they were in the cradle. If you ask me it's the cinema that's the killer.'

'Or the internal combustion-engine . . .'

'Leastways, I shan't quit before my old man does . . .!'

There was quite a pleasant haze in the warm air of the lounge by the time Pauline Lammas appeared. She was not put out by it — on the contrary, she paused at the door to light a cigarette of her own. Taller and more robust than her mother, Pauline tended to plainness of feature. She had short, straw-coloured hair, greyish-blue eyes and a thickened nose, and made-up a good deal more than was necessary. She wore a black bodice-blouse and a green skirt.

Gently rose courteously when she entered. From her private cloud of smoke she quizzed him coolly.

'And – *you* are Chief Detective Inspector Gently, CID?'

Wooden-faced, Gently admitted it.

'Really . . . you're not a bit how I expected you to be. I'm afraid I'm going to be disappointed – do you mind?'

'Not essentially, Miss Lammas . . .'

'You see,' she hurried on, 'I visualized you as one of the younger school of detectives – the sort they make films about, or at least lean and hatchet faced and – and *intellectual* looking. But you aren't. You're just *paternal*. It's difficult to believe that you're a detective at all!'

Gently cleared his throat, but Hansom gave his harsh laugh.

'Don't worry, miss – he hates people to think he looks like a policeman!'

'Does he really? How strange!'

'He likes you to take him for a farmer or a commercial traveller!'

'*Ahem!*' coughed Gently loudly. 'I think perhaps we should get down to business . . . don't you?'

Hansom chortled to himself and kicked his large feet happily under the table. Pauline Lamas swept her bushy green skirt flat and sat down with precision timing.

'Now, Miss Lammas . . . I understand you were in Norchester all the Friday evening.'

'Yes, inspector. I'm playing Cordelia for the Anesford Players – our first night is a week today.'

'It is a pity, Miss Lammas, that this tragic circumstance should have intervened.'

A flicker of emotion twisted the corner of the young girl's mouth, but immediately she recovered her former brightness.

'It's not going to intervene, inspector. Daddy wouldn't have expected it.'

'You mean you still intend to play?'

'Of course – he would have wanted me to. Daddy was a Player himself. Hasn't anyone told you?'

'Naturally . . . if you feel it's your duty.' Gently shrugged. 'Miss Lammas, what time was your rehearsal on Friday?'

'At half-past seven, at St Giles' Hall.'

'Who is the producer of the Anesford Players?'

'John Playfair – he's the Drama Organizer. You can get him at his office in Pacey Road or his private address at 40 Birdcage Hill.'

'Thank you, Miss Lammas! You are correct in assuming that I shall need to get in touch with him. What time did the rehearsal end?'

'Oh, you know what they are, inspector! They go on till all hours. But I had to leave at twenty-past ten to catch my last bus.'

'In fact, you were at St Giles' Hall from the time the rehearsal commenced at seven-thirty until you left to catch your bus at twenty-past ten. Is that correct?'

'Perfectly correct . . . you've only to ask John Playfair. Or anyone else who was there.'

Gently nodded absently. 'And what time did your bus leave?'

'At ten thirty-five from Castle Paddock.'

'And arrived here?'

'At eleven o'clock. You get off at Wrackstead Turn.'

'How about the bus going?'

'I took the ten to seven.'

'Then would you be kind enough to tell me, Miss Lammas, what you were doing between the time you finished your early tea served at five-thirty and ten minutes to seven?'

There was the briefest of pauses, just sufficient to warn the alert Hansom that Gently had struck oil of some sort. Then Pauline Lammas laughed, only a fraction off-cue.

'Of course, inspector . . . on Friday night I took the early bus!'

'Why?' fired Gently.

'Why—? To do some shopping, I suppose.'

'What shops are open after six o'clock?'

'What shops? Oh . . . I don't know! It was window shopping.'

'You took an early bus, simply to window-shop?'

'Yes, why not?'

'When you are in town every day of the week?'

'One doesn't get much time, in business.'

'Why in fact did you come home at all, Miss Lammas? Wouldn't it have been easier for you to have had tea in the city and to have gone to the rehearsal from there?'

Pauline Lammas laughed again, this time well on cue.

'You *are* a detective, aren't you, inspector? It wouldn't do to have any secrets from you!'

'This isn't answering the question.'

'But it scarcely needs answering. I came home not long after lunch. Friday afternoon is slack and I am a privileged employee . . . why are you trying to catch me out, inspector?'

Gently grunted and struck a light for his extinguished pipe.

'I shouldn't have to remind you that this is a serious business, Miss Lammas . . . we want the truth, and not a special selection from it. I put it to you that you haven't given me the real reason why you took the earlier bus to town on Friday evening.'

A sullen look crept over the girl's face. 'And if *I* put it to *you*, inspector, that my real reason had nothing to do with my father's death – won't that be sufficient answer?'

'You must let me be judge of that.'

'I'm sorry, but I don't propose to.'

'That may be unfortunate, Miss Lammas. It may lead me to attach more importance to the circumstance than it deserves.'

'Then you'll simply have to, inspector, won't you?'

Gently puffed silently a few moments, aware of a delighted Hansom at his elbow. Pauline Lammas lit a second cigarette from her first. She reached forward to stub out the butt in the ashtray on the table and Gently noticed a slight tremor in her well-groomed hand.

'You were very fond of your father, were you not, Miss Lammas?'

'I understood Daddy. We always got on together.'

'Your brother, on the other hand, was antagonistic towards him.'

'Paul is a spoiled little fool. It was Mother who set him against Daddy. He's been spoiled and pampered until he's no good to himself or anyone else.'

'There was some trouble about him refusing to enter the business, wasn't there?'

'Dear me yes! It was quite typical of Paul. He knew Daddy wanted so badly to have him in the business and to change the name to "Lammas & Son Ltd." – he could have walked right into a partnership as soon as he left the Grammar School. But Paul do what was expected of him? Paul soil his hands with dirty commerce? Good heavens, he was a poet – he wasn't going to waste his time in bourgeois money-grubbing!'

'You supported your father, of course?'

'He needed someone to support him, inspector! His life here has been hell ever since I can remember. He was nobody in this house, except an intruder. If it hadn't been for us I feel pretty sure he would have got out long ago. But that wasn't his way. He hung on and tried to make something out of it. I think it was the dust-up with Paul that finally broke his heart.'

'You were not surprised, then, to learn that he was apparently planning to disappear?'

Pauline Lammas hesitated. 'No,' she said defiantly. 'I wasn't.'

Gently's mild glance sought her eyes.

'Would it be too much to say, Miss Lammas, that you were quite well aware of what he had in mind?'

She tried valiantly to out-stare him, but there was something peculiarly undeniable about Gently's glances. Her eyes dropped to the table.

'It would be a great deal too much.'

'How long have you worked at the business?'

'Just over a year.'

'During that year, Miss Lammas, your father must slowly have been realizing his assets. The stock was being progressively reduced, employees dismissed, items such as trucks and vans being sold, and towards the end, at all events, business being turned away. Can you truthfully say that all this went on without your noticing it?'

'I did – but he didn't tell me why he was doing it!'

'And you didn't ask him, though it happens that you are one of the minor shareholders?'

'That's only a form, as you know!'

'Or warn your mother, the other minor shareholder?'

'It doesn't *mean* anything – we had only a share each so he could form the company!'

'Setting that aside, Miss Lammas, wouldn't you have naturally asked him as his daughter, or have been told without asking?'

'I tell you he didn't tell me – neither did I ask!'

'At least you will not deny that you had strong suspicions.'

She bit her lips. 'No. I guessed what it was about.'

'And you saw fit to keep it to yourself, not even exchanging a word with him about it?'

'Why?' she broke out. 'Why are you bothering about all this? It's the murder that matters, not how poor Daddy was planning to run away!'

Gently tapped his pipe with a stubby forefinger and sighted the stem at her.

'As a result of that plan, Miss Lammas, your father had a very large sum of money with him when he was murdered . . . we are naturally interested to know who was aware of the fact.'

There was silence. Pauline Lammas hung her head sullenly, an obstinate set to her mouth. Hansom tilted his chair back and gave his best impression of being bored. The Constable's pencil hovered dutifully beside the last crossed stop.

'Well?' prompted Gently.

Pauline Lammas hunched her shoulders. 'I've said I guessed. What more can I say? You *know* it couldn't have been me that killed Daddy.'

'I'm not suggesting it . . . but I think you could be a little more frank.'

'If I knew anything that would help I would tell you.'

'It is your place to tell us everything, not just what you think might help.'

'I *am* telling you everything! What else is it you want to know?'

Gently lowered his pipe and laid it on the table beside him.

'You must have known about your father and Miss Brent . . . when did that affair begin?'

'Oh . . . she was engaged soon after I went there. I really can't tell you when Daddy first took a serious interest in her.'

'It was a serious interest, was it? I mean, it wasn't merely a flirtation?'

'Oh no. It was the real thing. If only he'd found someone like that to start with!'

'I take it you approved?'

'Yes. I was pleased about it. Daddy deserved a little compensation for all he had to put up with.'

'You did not see it as your duty to warn your mother, for instance?'

'Good heavens no! What right had she to know, after the way she had treated him? And what sort of a daughter would I have been to him if I had told her? You don't understand, inspector!'

'Would it have been possible for her to find out?'

'I don't think so, or we should have heard about it.'

'What about the other members of the office staff?'

'I suppose our head clerk, Mr Page, may have guessed something. But Daddy was always very careful in front of them.'

'He wasn't so careful in front of you.'

She drew back her head proudly.

'He knew he could *trust* me.'

Gently brooded a moment.

'They used to go away together, did they?'

'Away? No – never! He used to take her out sometimes, but it was only to do a show at Starmouth or somewhere. He might have been recognized in Norchester.'

'How did they get to these places?'

'He'd drive her in the Hillman the traveller uses.'

'Never in his own car?'

'No. It would have gone straight back to Mother through Hicks.'

'But Hicks knew Miss Brent, did he?'

'I suppose he'd seen her. He used to drive us to and from the office.'

'But he wasn't friendly with her?'

'No, that's ridiculous! Linda is a cultivated woman. Hicks is just a – well, a yokel.'

'Hmn.'

Gently seemed lost for a short spell, as though his mind had wandered elsewhere. He picked up a pencil and doodled vaguely with it on his pad. Then, just as Hansom was beginning to jiffle, he asked:

'If your father didn't go away with Miss Brent, where *did* he go . . .?'

'My father—?' Pauline Lammas stared uncomprehendingly.

'Yes . . . just lately he'd made some mid-week trips somewhere. If they were on business you ought to know about them.'

She shook her head. 'He didn't always tell us.'

'You agree that he made these trips?'

'Oh yes. Why not?'

'And Miss Brent did not accompany him?'

'No. She was at the office as usual.'

'Did he use his car?'

'. . . No. I think he went by train.'

'And neither you nor the office knew where he went . . . he was just On Business if anyone inquired?'

'If you don't believe me, inspector, you can always check at the office.'

Hansom scribbled a little sketch on his pad, tore it off and pushed it across to Gently. It depicted a cottage with a 'To Let' notice, and the 'To Let' crossed out. Hansom grinned modestly all over his face. Gently crumpled it up and let it drop in the ashtray.

'Well, Miss Lammas . . . that seems to be all we can accomplish for the moment.'

'Thank you, inspector. I wish I could have been more helpful.'

'So do I, Miss Lammas,' returned Gently without expression, 'but we do our best, don't we . . .?'

She flashed him her brightest smile and made an impeccable exit.

'Har, har,' said Hansom unhumorously, 'she was always a one for acting, indeed to goodness!'

Gently got up and went over to the french windows. 'But it's the casting that's the problem, isn't it . . .?'

'What about my little house – that explains a few things.'

'It might, if it exists.'

'How do you mean – if it exists! It's as plain as the nose on your face. Lammas is working on a vanishing act, so he buys himself a hideaway. His little train trips are spent furnishing it and maybe establishing a nice new character for himself.'

'And that's where we'll find the secretary?'

'You can bet your life on it!'

'Then why hasn't she come forward? She must have read the newspapers.'

Hansom waved his hands exasperatedly. 'Can't you use some imagination? She's probably sitting tight with the deeds of the place and maybe the cash too. Handing them over isn't going to resurrect Lammas – so what would you do, chum?'

Gently nodded a grudging assent. 'But if he sent her off with the cash, what motive had Hicks to bump him off?'

'He needn't have known the cupboard was bare. And I'm still not convinced there wasn't anything between him and the secretary.'

'But why did Lammas send for Hicks – if he did? He knew full well that whatever Hicks was party to would go straight back to Mrs Lammas.'

'*If* he did – that's the number one query!' Hansom brooded brilliantly. '*If* he did, then my guess is he was aiming to lay a false trail of some sort, like getting Hicks to take him some place where the hideaway wasn't.'

'Why should he bother?'

'Well, he seems to have been a pretty crafty planster so far.'

Gently shook his head with slow decision. 'The bit that doesn't fit in anywhere is the week he spent on the yacht . . . it just wasn't necessary on the facts we've dug up. His false trail started at the beginning of that week. What made him hang around the neighbourhood till the end of it?'

'Christ! Let him be human. He was having a honeymoon.'

'There were safer places to do that. It was a risk, however little he was known.'

'Perhaps that's why he sent for Hicks. Someone recognized him, so he had to cover his tracks again.'

'No . . . it doesn't sit square in the picture. We haven't got the reason yet.'

Hansom sniffed meanly and tore off a light for his

second whiff. 'Anyway, you won't mind me following up this hideaway angle just in case I'm being right somewhere?'

Gently grinned and blew out his colleague's match.

'It'll keep you out of mischief, won't it?' he replied.

CHAPTER SIX

P AUL LAMMAS WASN'T quite so petite as his
mother, but otherwise he was very, very like.

Dark, slender, he had the same big brown eyes and
fragile features, the same low, clear voice. And he moved
the same way, quickly and nervously, though always with
grace. The difference about him was difficult to pin down.
It was something in his manner rather than his appearance.
Mrs Lammas struck one as icy, Paul as though he
concealed a secret fire; her emotions were rigidly
controlled, his seemed at the point of spilling over. He was
wearing a dark-red linen sports shirt with ash-grey jacket
and trousers in gaberdine. His rope-and-canvas sandals
matched his shirt. He came into the room so quietly that
nobody could have sworn to seeing him enter.

'I am Paul Lammas. My sister informed me that you
were ready to question me.'

Gently turned round from the veranda where he had
been basking and watching the yachts.

'That was kind of her. I hadn't really made up my
mind.'

'If you want Mother I will go and fetch her.'

'No, don't bother. I daresay your sister knows best.'

He came back out of the veranda. Paul Lammas stood quite still, watching.

'Sit down, Mr Lammas, if you please . . .'

'Thank you. But I'd rather stand.'

'We may be some little while, you know . . .'

'All the same I'd rather stand, if it isn't breaking immutable regulations.'

Gently shrugged and seated himself heavily at the table. He seemed in no hurry to begin. He emptied his pipe in the ashtray, filled it slowly and expertly, sucked it once or twice to test the packing and then lit it at some length. Even then he appeared to hesitate before getting down to business.

'You're a poet, they tell me . . .?' he remarked, patting down the ash on the pipe with a yellowed forefinger.

The young man flushed.

'I don't see how that comes into it.'

'It doesn't; there's nothing culpable about it. I'm just one of those people who read poetry from time to time.'

Paul Lammas looked at him as though he thought it unlikely.

'Of course, you wouldn't have seen anything of mine. It's only been published in *Panorama* and the *Eastern Daily Post*, and a little book I brought out myself.'

'Did it sell?' inquired Gently naively.

'I suppose you'd say it didn't – and judge it entirely from that point of view!'

'Oh, I don't know . . . the provinces are hardly the place to peddle poetry.'

'It's not a question of whether it sells, anyway. And one doesn't *peddle* poetry, as you're kind enough to put it.'

'Then how do people like me get to see it?'

'They don't – and it doesn't matter. Creation is the only thing that signifies.'

Gently nodded. 'I heard it in a play somewhere . . . but the author wasn't sad because it pulled in some audience.'

'That's the cynical view one would expect!'

'It struck me that the other view was the cynical one . . . but we'd be all day arguing about it!'

He felt in his baggy pocket and pulled out a small package, which he laid on the table. Hansom rocked back out of a fit of ennui to examine it. But Gently left it wrapped up in front of him.

'Well . . . we'd better check off that motorbike ride of yours, I suppose. Why aren't you at Cambridge, by the way?'

'I was sick, Mother wanted me at home.'

'You look all right now. When did you come home?'

'Last Saturday week . . . she sent the car for me.'

'Did you see your father?'

'No. I didn't get here till tea-time.'

'Right you are . . . now tell me about the ride.'

Paul Lammas straddled his feet on the deep-piled carpet and launched into his account without hesitation. He had spent the day lying in the hammock in the garden. After tea he had felt restless and had got out his motorcycle. At first he had thought of going to the coast, but it was getting a bit crowded at this time of the year, so instead he struck inland. He gave rough details of his route. He had set out at about seven and got back at about a quarter to ten. He had been as far as Cheapham, which was thirty miles away.

Gently jotted down some figures.

'It gives you an overall average speed of about twenty-two miles an hour . . . did you stop for a drink, or were you just taking it easy?'

'I was riding for pleasure, not trying to break my neck. You know what the side roads are like.'

'But you didn't stop for a drink or anything like that?'

'No, I *didn't* stop for a drink. I am not in the habit of drinking at public houses.'

Gently clicked his tongue. 'And you a poet, too! But you remembered your route well.'

'I happen to know the roads around here.'

'Then you'll be able to go through it again . . . on this Ordnance Survey.'

He pulled open the package which had so much intrigued Hansom. It contained a brand-new one-inch OS map of the district.

'Here we are . . . where we're sitting . . . and there's Cheapham over on the other side. Now you can show us properly, Mr Lammas.'

The young man came up to the table slowly but quite confidently. He picked up Gently's pencil as though to demonstrate his complete unconcern. If there was a slight hesitation at this fork or that, it was no more than might be expected of one retracing the precise route of a casual evening run.

'There you are – as near as I remember.'

'Thank you, Mr Lammas . . . it must have been a pleasant little ride.'

'I pride myself on knowing the quieter parts of Northshire.'

'I see you took the Tackston road . . . I've an idea I went fishing there many years ago. Did you see any anglers as you crossed the bridge on Friday?'

'There were two or three. I stopped on the bridge to watch them.'

'Were they having good sport?'

'I suppose so. I wasn't there long.'

Gently sighed and brought something else out of his pocket.

'Here,' he said, 'why don't you read your papers? They started demolishing that bridge a week ago . . . the Tackston road has been closed since Monday.'

Paul Lammas flushed violently and dropped the pencil from his fingers.

'You're trying to trap me – that's what you're doing! Mother warned me what you would do—!'

'Mrs Lammas warned you?' Gently's eyebrows rose. 'Have you been discussing what story you should tell us?'

'It *isn't* a story!'

His voice rose to a scream.

'I can't remember exactly – why should I remember? I wasn't thinking what I was doing just riding along with my mind a blank!'

'Then why did you pretend to remember?'

'To satisfy you! That's all – that's why! I knew you wouldn't be satisfied if I said I didn't remember. It's beyond your comprehension to understand that one may be doing a banal thing like riding a motorcycle, with one's mind miles away. So I had a guess at it. I tried to think where I probably went. I didn't believe you would be so pathologically suspicious as to set a trap over such a simple little thing. But it's a lesson to me, I assure you. I shall think twice what I tell to policemen in the future!'

'Hmn.'

Gently regarded him stolidly.

'At least it's a curious way to ride such a lethal instrument as a motorcycle . . . where did you really go?'

'To Cheapham – only I don't remember how I got there.'

'It wouldn't have been by way of Ollby – with your mind miles away?' struck in Hansom sardonically.

'It's the *truth*!' screamed Paul, turning on him wildly. 'It *is*, I tell you – it *is*!'

'All right, all right!' Gently waved a pacific hand. 'There's no need to get worked up about it, Mr Lammas . . . if you say it's the truth we'll duly note the fact. Now why not sit down and try to be a little more accurate and helpful?'

Paul glared at him in defiance for a moment, but he was trembling violently and needed the seat. He sat down. Gently gave him time off while the map was refolded.

'Do you smoke, Mr Lammas?'

'What has that got to do with it?'

'I was going to offer you a fill, if you smoked a pipe.'

'Thank you, but I only smoke my own brand!'

Gently shrugged and slipped the map back in his pocket.

'Getting back to Friday night . . . you arrived in ahead of your mother, I understand.'

'I did. I hope it wasn't a criminal act.'

'How long ahead of your mother?'

'About four or five minutes. She had gone for a run to Sea Weston – she *often* goes for a run to Sea Weston!'

'I wasn't asking for details of your mother's movements, Mr Lammas . . . she joined you here in the lounge, did she not?'

'I suppose so.'

'What happened then?'

'We talked, of course. I daresay we smoked and read.'

'Of what did you talk?'

'I really don't remember.'

'Come, come, Mr Lammas . . . the servants have ears too.'

Paul glanced at him with sudden apprehension, but the words that came to his lips were repressed.

'We know there was a row . . . I'm asking you what it was about.'

'But there wasn't a row – that's absolute moonshine!'

'Call it what you like.'

'I tell you there was nothing of the sort! Mother and I have never rowed in our lives. What on earth should we have rowed about? It's a lot of kitchen tittle-tattle!'

Hansom swooped forward in his chair. He wasn't even pretending to be bored.

'Look . . . in words of one syllable! Suppose you went out and bumped off your old man. Suppose your mother had a hunch and tailed you to Ollby. Suppose she worked on the chauffeur and got him to act the fall-guy. Wouldn't that add up to a conversation piece when you next got together?'

Gently had rarely seen such ghastly pallor in a human face. The young man's eyes seemed almost black against the mask of white.

'You don't . . . you *can't* . . . believe that!'

'Why not? It fits the facts!'

'But it's ludicrous . . . you *can't*!'

He was swaying as he sat. Every moment Gently expected to see him pitch forward on to the floor. But he didn't. He fought it off. With his small mouth compressed till it was practically invisible, he forced the colour back into his cheeks. It was an effort of pure will.

'What you say is untrue . . . there isn't a grain of truth in it!'

'We're not saying there is.' Gently threw a fierce glance at Hansom. 'The inspector was merely emphasizing that this is a case of homicide and that prevarication may be dangerous. He had no other intention.'

Hansom made a face and rocked back into neutrality.

'But we would still like an answer to the question . . . what was the occasion of the difference with your mother on Friday night?'

'I've told you; there wasn't any difference.'

'Then the servants were lying to us?'

'Yes. If they say there was. Lying or using their imagination too much.'

'What do you mean by that?'

'We talked, didn't we? We discussed the traffic and the way Sea Weston was being spoiled by trippers.'

'Then why did you not say so when I first asked?'

'You didn't give me time to remember – you started accusing us of having a row.'

Gently sighed and reached out for a fortifying peppermint cream.

'Your memory is certainly an oddity . . . but then, I'm not used to dealing with poets! Let's try some background stuff. What was Hicks doing all day?'

'What he usually does.'

'Go on. Tell me.'

'Well . . . he washed the cars down – drove my sister to the office – did some shopping in town for Mother. In the afternoon I imagine he was taking it easy. Pauline caught a bus back and nobody else called him out.'

'You saw a lot of him, I'm told.'

'I did, but I didn't persuade him to kill my father.'

'That is not the suggestion, Mr Lammas. It would be helpful if you confined yourself to answering a question. Was Hicks on good terms with your father?'

'Nobody was on good terms with him.'

'Wasn't there some question once of Hicks being dismissed?'

'There was no question about it – Mother engaged Hicks. Otherwise he would have gone long since and the cook and the maid with him. My father's authority here was fortunately limited.'

'I don't have to ask what was your own attitude towards him.'

Paul shrugged.

'I'm not hiding it, am I? He wasn't wanted here and he knew it.'

'That matter of going into the business . . .'

'Yes – that was a spoke in his wheel he didn't forget! I can't make you understand. You're simply policemen and it wouldn't make sense to you. There are two powers in this world, one for beauty and one for ugliness. My father stood for ugliness, sordidness – spiritual blindness, if you know what I mean. And into this he would have drawn me. Oh yes! It was to be a matter of course. I was his son, and he could do what he liked with me. As if, for one moment, I should have dreamed of burying my life in the filthy, parasitic business of wholesaling!'

'Parasitic? It offended your political principles?'

The young man glanced at him jeeringly. 'All politics are a racket . . . of course, my *father* was a politician! A Liberal, mind you – the height of bourgeois timidity. He was too soggy to be a thorough-going Tory or a thorough-going Communist, or even a Socialist. Just a milk-and-water Liberal!'

'That's not so terrible . . . I should probably be one myself if I wasn't a policeman. Did your father put any pressure on you to enter the business?'

'Moral pressure – he hadn't anything else. Oh yes, he argued himself black in the face!'

'Did he threaten to cut you out of his will or anything like that?'

'Why should that bother me? Mother and I have plenty of money.'

'But did he?'

'Yes, I suppose so.'

'And what else?'

'There was nothing else he could do.'

'You are a minor, Mr Lammas. Your father had certain powers. I should be interested to know, for instance, what was to have been done about your National Service . . . now, I take it, comfortably postponed until you leave Cambridge?'

The flush crept back into Paul's cheek.

'I wouldn't have done it . . . I shan't ever do it. I happen to have a weak heart. I can get a specialist's certificate to prove it any time I have to.'

'Is that quite true, Mr Lammas?'

'Yes, it is! Mother's specialist promised to give me one!'

Gently folded his hands under his chin and gazed at the young man for a long moment.

'Isn't it possible, Mr Lammas . . . isn't it just possible . . . that your father threatened to query that certificate and to ensure that you *did* do your National Service, if you persisted in refusing to enter the business? Would that be why you went to Cambridge and postponed your career as a poet with a private income . . .?'

Like a lighting switch the flush ebbed away into pallor. Paul's lips trembled and moved without words, and he began to sway again in his chair.

'And of course,' added Gently thoughtfully, 'the same problem would arise again in two years' time, wouldn't it? Only this time there wouldn't be Cambridge to run to.'

'It's a lie . . . a downright lie!'

The lips articulated at last.

'You're making something up and trying to pin it on me . . . there isn't a word of truth, you can't prove there is!'

'You mean that your father is dead and that your mother will support you?'

'You're trying to give me a motive . . . it's ridiculous! Nobody would listen!'

'It's a possible motive . . . for a young man of your temperament. And you had the opportunity. What were you doing down here – in *this particular week?*'

'I told you – I was sick!'

'With what?'

'My heart was giving trouble—'

'What doctor did you see?'

'I haven't seen one – I have to rest, that's all!'

'By making trips on your motorcycle?'

'That was Friday, I was feeling better—'

'And your mother raised no objection.'

'Why should she – she *knew* I was feeling better!'

Gently paused like a stalking tiger.

'The name "Beretta" – what does *that* mean to you?'

'"Beretta" . . .! I never heard of it!'

Gently plunged once more into his capacious pockets and threw something heavy and metallic clattering on to the table. It was a small automatic pistol with a slightly projecting barrel and a hook-shaped catch at the base of the grip.

'There – that's a Beretta – a Beretta .22. Are you sure you've never seen one – here – in this house?'

Trembling till his teeth almost chattered, Paul leaned forward and with an effort picked up the gun.

'It's – it's my father's gun . . . of course I knew he had it!'

'Go on.'

'It was a year or more ago . . . there'd been some burglaries. The police gave him a licence. I've seen him clean it in the garage.'

'And you knew where he kept it?'

'No! God help me . . . never, never!'

'Do you know why it's important?'

'Why should I – nobody's been shot!'

'Oh yes they have, Mr Lammas – your father was shot through the head.'

The pistol dropped with a thud on to the carpet. The young man slithered down his chair and had to seize the sides to prevent himself from falling off.

'I didn't do it!'

His voice was a whisper.

'I didn't – *I just didn't do it!*'

Gently signed to Hansom, who was sitting completely enthralled with the proceedings. Hansom picked up the gun impatiently and shored Paul up in his chair again. Gently arranged the gun neatly in front of him and waited.

'I tell you I didn't . . .'

'We heard you the first time, Mr Lammas.'

'But you're trying to frame me with it!'

'No.' Gently shook his head.

'Then what's it all about?'

'It's about the truth you haven't told us.'

Paul bit his small, shapely lips and stared unseeingly at the gun on the table. Then his eyes rose slowly and fastened themselves on Gently. And there they rested, dark, frightened, but entirely determined.

'Very well,' murmured Gently, 'that's all there is to it . . . tell your mother to come in, will you? I expect she isn't far away.'

The young man pulled himself to his feet. He left without another word.

'I like that boy!' exclaimed Hansom joyously. 'Yes – I like that boy!' He flipped a half-crown into the air and then held it out to Gently. 'What do you say – little Paul against the field? What are you going to give me?'

Gently grinned and pushed the half-crown away.

'I only once bet on a case and that time I won . . . which is why I never collected.'

'Hell!' exclaimed Hansom. 'When did *I* start being a suspect?'

CHAPTER SEVEN

MRS LAMMAS DIDN'T appear immediately, which suggested certain things to the sagacious Inspector Hansom. Gently merely shrugged and got up to wander round the room. It was a room worth wandering around. If ever taste and expense had combined to create the ideal room to overlook a broad, this was that room. In size it was about thirty feet by fifteen. Along the south side ran a range of deep windows opening on to the wide, thatch-sheltered veranda. The colour scheme was pale yellow and green; yellow, reeded wallpaper, a carpet of restrained turquoise and furniture in straw-coloured wood upholstered in flowered turquoise silk. And it was glorious furniture. In it the genius of Scandinavia had been tempered with a Sheratonian delicacy, a feminine exquisiteness. It made Gently feel quite dangerous as he picked his way through it. On the walls were a few original pictures, a pair of Seagos, an Arnesby Brown, a Peter Scott and a group of six watercolours of Broadland birds by Roland Green. And from any point in the room one turned to the long vista of the sun-flashed broad with its low, reed-and-carr fledged shores, its lily-nestling islets, its geometry of dream-moved sails . . .

Also, thought Gently, there were pike in that broad . . . and tench and bream and roach and perch . . .

He shook his head sadly and put a light to his stone-cold pipe.

There were heavy steps climbing up to the veranda. It was Dutt coming back from his horticultural assignment.

'Well, Dutt . . . how are crimes down there?'

Dutt smiled all over his cockney face and held up what appeared to be a toffee-tin.

'I got the goods, sir – just take a butcher's into this!'

Proudly he opened the tin and displayed the contents. It contained some greasy rag, a small wire-handled brush, a bottle of Rangoon oil and three spent .22 shells.

'Fahnd it in the garage, I did – just sitting on the bench, as large as flipping life!'

'We know, Dutt. He used to clean it there.'

'Know sir, do we?' Dutt was a trifle dashed. 'But this here's the proof, sir – the shover *must* have known about his nib's pop-gun!'

'So does everyone else, Dutt. Don't tell me the gardener didn't know.'

'Well, now you mention it! But I don't think *he* had anythink to do with the job.'

'He's got an alibi?'

'Yessir. He's the local sexton, sir. They buried an old girl called Micklewright on the Friday and natural-like, sir, they went and drank her health afterwards. He ain't

82

sure wevver he got back Friday night or Saturday morning, but if it ain't the one then it must be the other.'

'That sounds a fairish sort of alibi, Dutt.'

'What I thought, sir.'

'And what about that jerrican?'

'Yessir. It come from the garage all right. The gardener says as how he used it to keep his weed-killer in and right upset he was 'cause someone had knocked it off.'

'Weed-killer, eh? There's something a bit macabre about this gardener! I suppose he didn't tell you when he first noticed the jerrican was missing?'

'No, sir. I asked him that particular. But this is the rum thing, sir – he swears blind it'd gone some time before Friday. He thought the shover had swiped it, but the shover said he hadn't. Then he tackles Mr Paul, who's always in and out wiv his motorbike.'

'And Mr Paul gave him a rude answer?'

'Very rude, sir . . . shocking.'

Gently clicked his tongue. 'It would be interesting to know just *when* that jerrican disappeared.'

'Looks like it wasn't an off-the-cuff murder,' sniffed Hansom.

'But who would know in advance that they'd have a chance of burning the body in the yacht? How did they *know* that Lammas was going to take the yacht up Ollby Dyke and that he'd be alone?'

'Well they did, didn't they?' retorted Hansom irrefutably. 'He couldn't have been so darned smart, after all.'

83

'Unless, of course . . .'

'Unless what?'

'Unless it was Lammas himself who took the jerrican away.'

Hansom stared at him incredulously for a moment, then he broke out into sarcastic laughter.

'Har, har – very funny! I know a couple of dozen types who'd lay on a cremation for themselves – especially when they were just going to be knocked off!'

'No – wait a bit . . . that's not the point. You're looking at it from the wrong angle. There are other things one can do with petrol besides using it to cremate bodies.'

'Such things as?'

'Well . . . such things as running petrol engines, for example.'

'Petrol engines! He could get his tank filled every mile or two on the Broads.'

'I know he could . . . on the Broads.'

The master-brain of Hansom worked slowly, but exceedingly well. He had the point in three seconds, starting from scratch.

'Yeah . . .! Now I'm with you! Boy oh boy, that's a fancy idea if you like! And he'd got the right sort of boat for the job – she wasn't big, but she'd got the depth for sea-going. And he'd dropped the femme. And the weather was set fair . . . we're on to something, I tell you! This is the real Mackay!'

'Of course, he would need a motive of some sort . . .'

'Smuggling!' yipped Hansom. 'What do you say to that?'

'Smuggling what . . . *out* of the United Kingdom?'

'What can you smuggle . . . gold! That's the answer. And that's why he cashed in – to buy himself a shipment!'

Gently smiled and shook his head, but the enraptured Hansom wasn't easy to shake free from an idea.

'It explains the whole shoot – why he hung around here and everything! You've only got to take it from the beginning and work through. He wanted more money – eight thousand wasn't enough to disappear on – so he arranges to run some gold – it won't come till the Friday – he cruises around till then, packs the girl off to the hideaway and goes up the Dyke to rendezvous with his gold!'

'What about the chauffeur . . .?'

'He must have been on to it.'

'You couldn't make him the gold-merchant, just to tidy the loose ends?'

Hansom snorted indignantly and bit the end off a cigar.

'All right, Mr Cleverdick . . . let's hear your version?'

'I haven't got a version . . . I was just noting a fact.'

Hansom lit the cigar bitterly and blew smoke all around himself. The real trouble with Gently, he thought, was his entire lack of forensic imagination . . .

Dutt coughed confidentially. ''Nother fact, sir, if you don't mind . . . on account of we had a warrant I takes the liberty of ascending to the shover's quarters, which are above the garage.'

'Any luck, Dutt? Any letters?'

'Nothink, sir. Just two from his aunt. And a lot of old football coupons which never won tuppence.'

★   ★   ★

85

A cloud drifted over the sun as Mrs Lammas entered. It was as though nature had conspired to put a dramatic point on the event. She paused in the doorway, delicately sniffing the alien smell of Hansom's cigar. Her cool gaze ran disapprovingly over the moved furniture and the policemen rising to their feet. Then it fell on the table and the automatic which lay there. And she swept forward with a sort of withering grandeur.

'Before we go any further, inspector, I should like to know by what right you have entered my husband's bedroom and removed that gun from the place where it was kept!'

Gently shrugged expressionlessly. 'We've entered nobody's bedroom, ma'am ... except the chauffeur's over the garage.'

'What nonsense, man! Do you take me for a fool? That gun was kept locked in a drawer beside my husband's bed. I have just been to examine it. It is unlocked and empty. If you didn't fetch the gun, then how did it get here?'

'I ought to explain.'

'You have exceeded your duty!'

'This gun, ma'am, is *not* your husband's.'

'I know full well that it *is*!'

Gently sighed, picked up the gun and handed it to her.

'Would you be kind enough to read the serial number, ma'am?'

'There is no need for me to read the serial number!'

'Is it' – he fumbled for a dog-eared envelope – 'is it 52 stroke 7981?'

'No, it is not – but what does that signify?'

'It signifies that it isn't your husband's gun . . . we obtained its serial number from the record of licences issued. This one was merely brought along to jog people's memories . . .'

Her sharp eyes bored into him, challenging every word.

'If it is as you say, then *where* is his gun?'

Gently extended his hands. 'We'd like to know, of course . . .'

'You told my son that Mr Lammas was shot. Is it your theory that he was shot with his own gun?'

'It's a fact that he was shot with a gun of that calibre.'

'Then does not a simple explanation arise – that Mr Lammas committed suicide?'

'Unfortunately it does not, ma'am. He was not shot where he was found.'

'I see.'

She sniffed again at the offending wreathes of Havana.

'Very well – we had better get down to this interview. I'm sorry if I was mistaken, inspector. You must understand that I am unused to invasions in this house, either from the police or other people. It is naturally upsetting to think that somebody is making free with one's property.'

Gently nodded soothingly and ushered her to her seat. Mrs Lammas sat down regally, folding her tiny hands in her lap.

'While we are on the subject, ma'am . . . has your husband's bedroom been cleaned recently?'

'It most certainly has. The rooms are run over daily.'

'The furniture, however . . . it wouldn't be polished daily?'

'It is polished once a week. I believe the maid is working there now.'

Gently nodded to Dutt, who rose immediately.

'You will have no objection, ma'am? It is essential that we inspect the bedroom.'

'I seem to have very little option, inspector. The best I can expect is to be informed of what I must consent to.'

Dutt departed at speed after being given the location of the bedroom. Gently toyed with the automatic for a moment before slipping it away in his pocket. Outside a little breeze had sprung up, whispering in the green reeds: it set the white sails slanting and weaving more purposefully.

'You had very little interest in your husband's business, Mrs Lammas, apart from being a minor shareholder?'

'I had none whatever, inspector. I very rarely went near the place. Whatever he did or did not do there was unknown to me.'

'Did your daughter never volunteer information?'

'My daughter is not the type to volunteer information. No doubt you have elicited the fact that she is to some degree estranged from me. I make no secret of it. She chose to be her father's sympathizer and that has set a certain distance between us.'

'I gather that there was a virtual separation between yourself and your husband, Mrs Lammas.'

'Yes. We have lived as strangers for most of our marriage. I do not propose to enter into details of this, inspector; they would not concern you. But you may take it that a state of isolation obtained as complete as may be expected in a single household.'

'You will forgive me for being frank . . . why was it you didn't separate formally?'

'Being equally frank, inspector, it was because my husband was useful to me.'

'Would you like to enlarge on that, Mrs Lammas?'

'Certainly, if you insist upon it. I am what you may call a person with a static attitude to life. I dislike changes and I dislike an ambiguous status. My husband was useful to me simply because he was my husband and once our relationship had been adjusted to my satisfaction I had no wish to have it altered. I will not deny that we clashed occasionally. You will have heard that he tried to assert his right to drag Paul into his business. But generally speaking we had learned to co-exist without perpetual friction and this I considered to be quite satisfactory. I trust I have answered your question?'

'Thank you, Mrs Lammas . . . and of course you knew nothing of your husband's association with Miss Brent?'

'Nothing whatever.'

'It would not have affected your attitude?'

Mrs Lammas made a swaying motion with her shoulder.

'Naturally, I would not countenance my husband being interfered with.'

'You would have taken some action, possibly?'

'I should. But it would hardly be a fair question to ask me *what*.'

Gently nodded but made no comment. Mrs Lammas glanced at him challengingly and then added:

'If I *had* known I might possibly have averted the tragedy which took place on Friday.'

'Possibly, Mrs Lammas.'

She shrugged her shoulders and was silent.

'With reference to that Friday . . .' Gently fixed his eyes on a passing half-decker. 'You were here all day until the evening?'

'Yes.'

'Your son went out on his motorcycle. Did he tell you he was going out . . . and where?'

'He told me he was going for a run. He was not certain where he would go.'

'I understand he suffers from a weak heart and that he was home from Cambridge, resting. Surely you would have had some objection to him taking out his motorcycle?'

Mrs Lammas permitted a smile to pass over her face.

'You musn't be too hard on Paul . . . my son is a poet. Certainly his heart is not strong, but that wasn't necessarily the reason for him being at home. The fine weather may have had something to do with it.'

'I see . . . and you had no suspicion of where he was going?'

'No. Why should I?'

'You followed him rather quickly, Mrs Lammas. It occurred to us that you might be keeping an eye on him.'

She laughed, a low, tinkling little laugh.

'Keep an eye on Paul! I wouldn't dream of such a thing, inspector.'

'It was purely coincidental?'

'If you can call it that. I had been preparing to go out since tea.'

Gently's eyes switched back from the half-decker, casually, carelessly.

'Then suppose he'd gone out to keep an eye on you, Mrs Lammas . . . what would you have to say to that?'

The laugh went out as though it had been doused with an extinguisher. Mrs Lammas sat very still and straight, the fingers of her two hands twining themselves together in her lap.

'Of course, I'm not saying he did. It was just the time factor that interested us.'

'You may rest assured, inspector —'

'He'd have no reason, would he? You were only going to Sea Weston.'

'The suggestion is ridiculous! What can you possibly have in mind?'

'And then he got back first — that doesn't look as though he were following you, does it?'

Mrs Lammas rose from her seat and drew herself up to her full stature in front of him.

'Inspector Gently, you will kindly tell me what you are insinuating or I shall refuse to answer another question!'

Gently shrugged and surveyed her Lilliputian indignation sadly.

'It's simple, ma'am . . . there was too much promiscuous driving going on.'

She sat down again. It was impossible to read her thoughts from her face. Like the features of a little statuette, they remained set and entirely devoid of expression.

'In effect, you are accusing us of telling lies?'

'Of being less than frank.'

'Oh, don't bother to pick your words! It amounts to exactly the same. Where did we go, then?'

'I'm hoping you will tell me.'

'I have told you – but you don't seem to be satisfied. If you expect a different tale you must give me time to concoct one.'

'The simple truth will do, ma'am.'

'Not, it would appear, for a policeman.'

An impasse seemed to have been reached and the intelligent Hansom jiffled and breathed stern smoke through his powerful nostrils. If only Gently knew when it was time to turn some heat on! But he remembered a former pointed glance of the chief inspector's.

'You see, ma'am, in a business like this we've got to have proof that people were where they say they were.'

'I am fully aware of that fact, Inspector Hansom.'

'And neither you nor Mr Paul have given us any.'

'For which we are much to be blamed. Have you any further comment?'

Hansom's eyes gleamed, but he struggled manfully against the instinct to bite off heads.

'We shall make stringent inquiries, ma'am.'

'I trust you will, in view of the exorbitant rates I pay.'

'We shall get the truth in the long run. It's in your own interest to make a clean breast now.'

'Your advice is kind, if not, perhaps, asked for.'

'It's not advice – I'm warning you!' bawled Hansom, goaded beyond discretion, 'this is a homicide inquiry – not a variation on Twenty Questions!'

Mrs Lammas turned cuttingly to Gently.

'Is this man strictly necessary to you, or is he here merely because of some ridiculous regulation?'

She wasn't going to alter her story. They went over it point by point, with special reference to Gently's large-scale map. It clicked home everywhere, like the movement of a Swiss watch. She had gone out. She had gone to Sea Weston. She had parked the car on a piece of waste ground. She had walked along the evening beach, where the tide had left the sand firm and smooth. And she had driven home again, to arrive just ahead of Paul. No, she hadn't spoken to anyone. She did *not* patronize the cafe or ice-cream bar at Sea Weston. Whether anyone who knew her had noticed her she could not say. Presumably the police would elicit that in the course of Inspector Hansom's stringent inquiries.

'And the disagreement you were alleged to have had with your son when you got home?'

'Entirely mythical, inspector. My servants are Welsh, you know, and inclined to use their imaginations.'

'They talked about it as though they were in no doubt.'

Mrs Lammas' tinkle of laughter was restored to office.

'You are too English, inspector . . . you don't understand Welsh people! Do you know what I honestly think is at the bottom of it?'

'I'd be glad to know.'

93

'Paul was giving an animated impression of a woman driver hogging the middle of the road. He raised his voice, of course. They must have heard it and assumed the rest.'

'They say it was going on for over an hour. Until your daughter came in, in fact.'

'They mean they were *talking* about it for over an hour, if I know anything about my own servants.'

Gently hunched his shoulders and stared at his pad full of scribbles.

'Leaving that, what happened to the photograph of your husband which used to stand on the bureau there?'

She looked sharply where he indicated and hesitated.

'I really couldn't say . . . unless he chanced to take it with him.'

'You agree that there was such a photograph?'

'Naturally! He was an inmate of the house. One was obliged to suffer certain evidences of it.'

'There would be other photographs . . . you have some you could show me?'

'I have one or two in my albums, though I should warn you that none of them are very recent.'

'All the same, I should be obliged to see them.'

Mrs Lammas rose and went over to a dainty little cabinet, from which she took four expensively bound snapshot albums. She brought them over to the table and laid them in front of Gently.

'This green one is the earliest; it was bought at Torquay. It should have quite a number of him.'

She flicked over a few of the pages. Then an expression of perplexity came into her eyes.

'Oh – but someone's taken them all out!'

'Mmn?'

'Look – here, and here . . . and here! There are only the mounts left. This is really going too far! I didn't particularly want them, but they *were* my property!'

She threw the green volume aside and picked up another. The anger growing in her countenance indicated what she found there.

'The absolute *pig!* These were *not* his to make away with. And I was on some of them – there were several with myself and Paul—!'

'You must remember that he was planning to disappear.'

'But this is criminal! Taking my photographs – they can never be replaced!'

'There'll be the negatives . . . what about them?'

She was back at the cabinet in a moment, rifling in a cardboard box and tossing film-wallets on to the carpet. But Lammas had apparently been thorough. She stamped on the floor with her tiny foot and hurled the box into a corner.

'I could *kill* him for this! I tell you I'm *glad* he's been murdered!'

'Come now, Mrs Lammas.'

'He knew it would hurt me . . . as though I should ever try to find out where he went!'

For a moment it looked as though she would burst into tears. Then she recovered herself and came slowly back to the table.

'Well, it didn't get him far. No, it didn't get him far!'

Gently nodded profoundly and made a sympathetic clicking noise.

'Something has just occurred to me.'

Mrs Lammas raised her head.

'Paul . . . he hated your husband. Wouldn't he hate anyone who tried to step into his shoes?'

What happened next was so unexpected that Hansom's jaw dropped open wide, while the Constable's pencil made a scribble like a seismograph recording.

Mrs Lammas screamed – a loud, blood-chilling scream. And having screamed, she rushed out of the room, slamming the door behind her.

'Glory O'Rory!' gabbled Hansom, 'what the blue blazes was all that about!'

Gently gazed at the slammed door stupidly. 'I'm not absolutely certain . . . just at the moment.'

'But what did you say to her to get a skirl like that?'

'Oh, something about Paul. I daresay it wasn't very important.'

Hansom looked at him darkly as he bent to find his cigar stump.

'All I can say is that you might give us a warning – that's all! Some of us have got nervous systems that haven't been chilled off with peppermint!'

Gently chuckled and gave his colleague a light.

CHAPTER EIGHT

THEY WEREN'T SO very busy, serving lunch at the Bulrush Café near the bridge. Later on in the week the novelty of using one's galley or cooking-locker would have worn off and things would liven up, but on Monday one still had a fund of enthusiasm.

Sitting in the window, you could watch the gay yachting crowd pass and re-pass. They were a hetero-genous lot, both sexes and all ages. Now it would be a noisy crowd of teenagers in open wind-cheaters and jazzy tasselled caps, now a family party, the father looking self-conscious with his legs sticking out of shorts. Or a young couple carrying a baby between them and looking very capable. Or vigorous young men in white jerseys and the beginnings of beards. Or a self-intent pair of honeymooners, or noisy children, or pretty girls.

Gently stared at them absently over his cup of coffee. He was aware of a certain irritation with himself. By now he ought to have been getting into the picture of this business – nothing would induce him to call the picture a theory! – there ought to have been a few broad strokes on the canvas indicating the final composition, however imperfect in detail.

But those strokes wouldn't come. Or rather, there were too many of them and they all looked slightly false.

Hansom, for instance, had run off half a dozen theories already, equally tenable . . . and equally unconvincing.

Yet there was a picture there behind it all. The bits and pieces he was digging up each fitted into a pattern of some sort, if only he could grasp what it was.

'There's that week on the yacht!' he grumbled for the fifth time, 'no man in his senses would have done a thing like that, unless.'

'Unless he had a damned good reason, sir,' added Dutt, trying to be helpful.

'Precisely! A damned good reason. And what good reason could he have?'

'Well, sir, like Inspector Hansom says . . .'

'Inspector Hansom is an ass, Dutt.'

'Yessir. My hopinion too, sir.'

'Hire yachts aren't allowed below Hightown Bridge at Starmouth. Lammas could never have got out to sea.'

'No sir. Though it was your idea about the jerrican, if you don't mind me saying so, sir.'

'Well I was wrong, Dutt . . . he took it for some other damned silly reason! Or else the chauffeur took it, or somebody planted it. But there weren't any sea-trips in mind, not in anybody's mind. That's something we can get into our thick heads!'

98

He felt better after this outburst. Perhaps it was the handsome Hansom who was getting on his nerves.

'Of course, Hansom's all right in his way . . .'

He finished his coffee and sat looking at the cup. On the balance, it has to be the chauffeur. There was nobody else with their neck showing quite as much. You could discount the woman. There were reasons why she might be lying low. But the chauffeur!

If they got his prints off the inside of that drawer there wouldn't be any doubts left. Hansom was sending his print man down straight away and there was a Constable left guarding the bedroom against any more polishers . . . innocent or guilty. There would be plenty of Hicks' prints in the garage. They could get them off tools, off doors, off the cars. And they could get Lammas' prints from the bedroom and from the office.

But supposing Hicks was wearing his gauntlets when he slipped that gun out of the drawer? And why wasn't the drawer locked . . . for it certainly hadn't been forced?

A tiny will-o-the-wisp lit up seductively in the corner of Gently's mind. That scream of Mrs Lammas' when he prodded her with the suggestion of another man! She wouldn't have been the first woman to fall for her chauffeur. Or was it the other way round – was it Hicks who had fallen for her and been made a tool of to square accounts with a defecting husband? Or an unwanted husband?

For a moment he let the idea dwell and expand in his brain.

It meant that Mrs Lammas knew her husband was on the yacht – to say the least. It also meant that she had caused him to get rid of Linda Brent before the end of the trip and had then lured him into the fastness of Ollby Dyke. Well . . . that wasn't impossible!

After that, it all fell into place like a jigsaw puzzle.

She slipped Hicks the gun and told him to stand by. She had driven down to the turn and ascertained that the *Harrier* had arrived. Then she phoned up from the call-box and Hicks had done the job for her, while a suspicious Paul lurked watching . . . perhaps had seen a rewarding embrace before the infatuated chauffeur was paid off and sent into hiding.

And the firing of the yacht, where did that fit in? If it was going to look like an accident, why arrange things so that Hicks took the blame?

That must have been Paul too! He had given a further twist to the plot. Ignorant that Hicks was cast for the fall-guy, he had visited the scene of the crime and, appalled at the obviousness of it, he had tried to cover up by creating a holocaust – almost erasing the identity of the victim in the process, which had been no part of his mother's plan.

Yes, they would certainly have plenty to talk over in that terrific hour before Pauline got back.

Triumphantly, Gently considered his coffee-cup solution in all its sweet reasonability. Then his inborn suspicion of a beguiling theory flooded back and swept it away.

He signalled to the waitress.

'Come on, Dutt, get rid of that coffee!'

'We going into tahn, sir?'

'Not us. We're getting that launch again.'

'But there's the office, sir ... ought to give it a butcher's.'

'Don't argue, Dutt. Hansom will see it doesn't run away. I want to know why Lammas spent that week on the *Harrier*, and I'm going to know it, if it means taking the Broads apart in six-inch sections!'

Dutt gulped his coffee resignedly.

Experience had taught him not to get between Gently and a hunch.

They had got a list from Old Man Sloley of all the yards where the *Harrier* had been seen on her tragic last cruise. Put together on a map, it looked distressingly like the average week's trip down the North River and its tributaries.

First Lammas seemed to have gone straight down to Eccle Bridge, the customary Ultima Thule of one-week yachtsmen. Then he had worked back upstream, exploring the Thrin to Hockling Broad and the Awl to Stackham Staithe. By the Friday night, if all had gone well, he would have been in a position to make an easy run to Sloley's Yard on the following morning.

Ten thousand yachtsmen did exactly the same between Easter and Michaelmas. What was he up to, if it hadn't been simply a pleasure cruise?

'Eccle Bridge – we'll go just where he went.'

Gently settled himself in the launch while Dutt took the helm. Rushm'quick cast off for them, a little disgruntled because he was being left out this time.

And then they were on their way . . . setting out exactly as the *Harrier* had set out nine days ago. In Gently's mind's eye the scrubby and much-used launch became a trim little auxiliary yacht, the hot afternoon turned to cool, mist-rising evening and the uncompromising figure of Dutt transmuted to a sophisticated beauty with straight black hair, a heart-shaped face and appealing eyes.

What had been in his mind that evening, as he throbbed across the pulk into the river? What did he see ahead of him past the slender mast and wire shrouds, over the symmetrical cabin-top, across the incurving decks with the quant laid one side and the mop the other?

'Never mind the speed limit . . . we've got to get a move on if we're to do the trip before dark.'

Dutt advanced the throttle-lever in its quadrant and they surged forward with a sudden thrust of power. There were irate shouts from the more law-abiding users of the river, but Gently seemed deaf to what was going on about him.

You had to go back further than that Friday evening. You had to go back twenty years or more, to an expensive hotel in Torquay of the thirties, when England was still an inviolable island and the Spanish Civil War a remote and somewhat perplexing incident. To that hotel had gone a beautiful young widow and her Welsh maid, a rich young widow, a young widow whose handsome officer-husband had been cruelly wrested from her a few weeks previously; not gloriously, not heroically, but as the result of a miserable scourge taken while carrying out useless routine duties in a coaling-station at the ends of the earth. Had she not a right to be bitter, that one? Had she not a right to complain at the cynical dispositions of a criminal providence? She had played the game by the rules and this had been her reward. She had asked only the common privileges of life and they had been snatched away with taunting laughter. Yes . . . she had grounds for bitterness, that beautiful and rich young widow!

But then there had been the other one, this confident businessman in his thirties, just beginning to enjoy his expanding circumstances. Wasn't it time he took a wife now, with his struggles all behind him? He could afford a wife, just as he could afford his new sports car. He had income and prospects, a handsome face, a trim figure . . . he was the sort of man that women put on a special voice for. But he would want a striking wife, just as he wanted a striking car. Soon he would be a councillor, one day probably mayor of his important provincial city – it helped, then, to have a wife who caught people's eye, who could hold her own with a duchess, or steal the picture from visiting royalty.

'Through the broad, sir?' enquired Dutt, nodding towards the Little Entrance.

'Don't be absurd, Dutt. As though he would parade right under his wife's nose!'

The launch continued to race downstream.

. . . And they had met, these two, the rich young widow and the pushing young businessman; they had met and decided that each had what the other wanted. She wanted another husband from life – a secure one this time, no being dragged away for sacrifice on the altar of Colonialism! And he wanted a superb specimen of the female, an outstanding woman – better still if well-bred, best of all if rich as well!

Wouldn't it be easy to imagine they were in love? Wouldn't it be easy to be reckless, when there were so many advantages in the match?

Only of course they weren't in love . . . that was something they had to discover later. In twenty-odd years. In two decades of slow division. Beginning – with what subtle modification of attitude did it begin? – in those hopeful, optimistic days of the early thirties; and ending when a disillusioned businessman, now no longer young, set out on a pleasure cruise with his secretary and all his realizable assets, heading for . . . *what?*

Gently's head shook slowly at the riotous jungle of the carrs. That was the crucial question which preceded all theory.

Only, it helped to keep that picture firmly in view. Unless it was there one could easily overlook a detail which might be the very one.

The launch slid up to the quay at Eccle and Gently jumped out without waiting for Dutt to make fast. Eccle Bridge was a little yachting community on its own, solitary in the wide marshes. A mile away was the village. Against the bridge clustered a boat-yard, a store, and at some distance a public house. For the rest it was a long, straight reach with good mooring on scrubby raised banks.

Gently poked his way into a boat-shed.

'Hi, you! Where's the gaffer?'

He was a tall, pale-eyed man of fifty, with a stoop and the calloused hands of a carpenter.

'Police . . . Chief Inspector Gently. Is it right that Sloley's *Harrier* moored here yesterday week?'

It was. The tall man had seen it himself. They had come in at about 7 p.m., when the moorings were already crowded, and tied up about halfway down the opposite bank.

'Did you know who it was?'

'No . . . it's the boats one notices.'

'You wouldn't know what they did that evening?'

The tall man simply shrugged.

It was the same at the pub – nobody knew Lammas, or knew if they'd seen him. Neither did they at the store, though they had a small piece of information for him.

'Of course I never knew Mr Lammas, but we've always done business with him. He's our wholesaler for a lot of lines . . . a lot of us deal with him round the Broads.'

'You do, do you? And who's his representative?'

'It's a traveller called Mr Williams.'

'Did you owe him any money?'

The store proprietor looked hurt.

'We keep a small account, naturally.'

'Nobody's tried to collect it – say first thing last Monday morning?'

But they hadn't, of course. That wasn't going to be the answer. Whyever else Lammas had spent his week

105

on the Broads, it wasn't to square up his odd accounts. At the same time . . . wouldn't there be *any* of his customers who knew him personally? And if so, wasn't it getting riskier and riskier, that honeymoon trip in the *Harrier*?

Gently sat like a carved idol beside his colleague all the way up the Thrin to Hockling. Lammas *couldn't* have kept that trip secret! Somewhere, sometime, he must have blundered into someone who would recognize him; even, perhaps, his own traveller. And then what had happened? Had they got on to Mrs Lammas? Or did they represent a mysterious extra element which so far hadn't come into his calculations?

And then once more . . . who knew better than Lammas the risk he was taking?

He might have spent that week anywhere else in the wide world!

'Stop here.'

They were passing the village of Petty Hayner.

Dutt fumbled with Old Man Sloley's list.

'It ain't one of the places, sir.'

'I know it isn't, but he'd stop for lunch, wouldn't he?'

And so it went on through the burning afternoon and the endless evening, stopping, checking, throwing out leading questions – and getting nowhere. It was only the *Harrier* people had seen. It was a chronic complaint with them – they noticed boats, but they didn't notice people. And, they would always add, if they had seen Lammas they wouldn't have known him . . . it was like inquiring for someone from another planet. Was it barely possible he had come through that week unscathed?

'Well, sir, it's been a nice little houting!' observed Dutt as they throbbed back upstream through the white smoke-mist. 'I never did get round to one of those holidays afloat before, but I reckon I've seen it all now, sir.'

Gently bit on the end of a dead pipe and reached automatically for a match.

'I've got an odd feeling, Dutt.'

'Yessir. That sun was bleeding fierce, sir.'

Gently grinned. 'I don't mean sunstroke! The feeling I've got is that I've learned something about this trip of Lammas', and I don't know what the blazes that something is.'

'You mean as how you can't see the wood, sir.'

'Exactly, Dutt – I can't see the wood.'

He scratched the match, which lit cheerily in the dank vapour curling past them.

'The further we go, the more it grows on me . . . but it's no use harping on it. What's this place we're just coming to?'

'Halford Quay, sir, 'cording to the map.'

'It isn't on the list, but we'd better give it a whirl.'

'You'll have covered the lot then, sir,' returned Dutt, with the merest tinge of bitterness.

Halford Quay was a popular spot. There were yachts and cruisers moored two deep all along its not-very-great expanse. At one end it was blocked by the gardens of a brightly-lit hotel, at the other chopped off by the cut-in of a boat-yard. Into this Dutt directed the launch. As they came alongside the staithe an elderly, bearded man in navy cap and sweater ambled across to them.

'Now don't yew know this is private properta . . . or dew yew think yew can buy petrol at this time of night?'

Gently shrugged and tossed him the painter.

'We shan't worry you long . . . and maybe you can tell us what we want to know.'

'Ah . . . maybe I can an' maybe I can't.'

He weighed up the launch with a professional eye, then cast a shrewd glance at the occupants.

'Tha's old Slola's boat, now, i'nt't? And I reckon I can guess who *yew* are without strainin m'self.'

Gently nodded briefly and climbed out on to the staithe.

'I was wonderin how long yew'd be gettin round here . . . thought that'd be a rummun dew yew missed me out!'

'You know why we're here then?'

'Blast yes – I can read the paper.'

'And you've something to tell us?'

'W'either I dew, or else yew don't hear it.'

Gently considered this ambiguous reply for a moment.

'What's your name?' he asked.

'Me! I'm Ole Sid Crow – Ole Sid'll dew round here.'

'You work at the yard here?'

'I dew, when I aren't idle.'

'Go on then – what've you got to tell us?'

Sid Crow came a little closer, as though afraid that a precious word might go astray.

'*He dropped her here* – tha's what I've got to tell yew. Now say I'm a blodda liar an' don't know what I'm talkin' about!'

He did know what he was talking about. He proved that up to the hilt. Of all the interviewees they had tackled on that trip, Sid Crow was the single one who knew Lammas by sight – he had worked at the Yacht Club on Wrackstead Broad and seen Lammas pull in there on his half-decker. And he could describe the clothes Lammas was wearing. And also Linda Brent.

The *Harrier*, it appeared, had moored at Halford Quay at tea-time on the Friday. The quay had been crowded then as it was now and she had tied up on the public side of the cut-in, right under Sid's nose. The two occupants had then proceeded to get tea. They had had it in the well, without any attempt at concealment. After tea they had smoked a leisurely cigarette, washed and put away the dishes, and a little later had gone ashore, Lammas carrying two suitcases and Linda Brent her handbag and plastic raincoat. They went in the direction of the bus stop. About ten minutes later Lammas returned alone. Without any hurry he made the yacht ship-shape, checked his petrol and then quanted her over to Sid's side for a fill up. And then he had set off upstream; time, about twenty to seven.

'You're sure it was to the bus stop they went?' queried Gently.

'W'no.' Sid Crow gave a deprecating twist with his shoulders. 'But tha's the way they went and there was a bus just about due.'

'What bus was that?'

'There's one go into Narshter at twenta past six, weekdas.'

'And what time would it get in at Norchester?'

109

'Bout seven – yew'd better ask them what go on it.'

Gently caught Dutt's eye with a meaningful look in it.

'There aren't any other buses round about then?'

'Nothin more till eight o'clock.'

'Thank you, Mr Crow. That's a useful piece of information.'

He paused a moment, puffing blue smoke into the tepid, misty air.

'Of course, when you heard what had happened to Mr Lammas you mentioned what you had seen to one or two people . . .?'

Sid Crow was disgusted.

'I'm old enough t'know when t'keep m'mouth shut – specialla when I knew that parta wa'nt his missus!'

'Then you didn't mention it to anyone?'

'Not the bit about the female.'

'But the bit about his being here on the *Harrier*?'

'W'yes – I told his missus.'

'You told *who*?'

'I told his missus – though mind yew, I woon't have done dew I ha'nt thought she knew about't alreada.'

Gently coughed over his sparking pipe. It was quite a few seconds before he got round to his next question . . .

'And *when* did you tell his missus?'

'Why, that verra same evenin'?'

She had driven up in her car at about a quarter past seven and parked it opposite the quay. Sid, alerted by what he had seen previously, had watched her with interest as she walked along the quay, obviously looking for the departed yacht. When she came to the end of the quay she had beckoned Sid across. She didn't know he recognized her.

110

'I'm looking for Mr Lammas on board the yacht *Harrier*. Have you seen him by any chance?'

Sid told her he had supplied the *Harrier* with petrol.

'His – er – wife, was she on board with him?'

'No mum. He was alone when he pulled in here.'

'He was on his way to Wrackstead, I suppose?'

'He certainla went off in that direction.'

Mrs Lammas had given Sid half a crown, gone back to her car and driven off again directly.

Gently sighed deeply at the end of this narration.

'And you weren't going to tell me this if I hadn't squeezed it out of you?'

Sid's weathered features wrinkled into a wink.

'Well, yew got to remember, ole partna . . . it was her what give me the half-crown.'

'Ahem!' coughed Dutt, 'don't you think we ought to take a statement, sir?'

It was dark when Gently sent the Wolseley bumbling down the lane to the cottage, but there were lights enough on the river bank. Besides the glimmer of lamps through houseboat windows there were two or three hurricanes placed at strategic points and in the space so illuminated an animated scene was enacting. As Gently switched off the engine the rollicking music of a concertina could be heard.

'Looks like they're having a spree, sir!' exclaimed Dutt, his cockney eyes brightening.

'And that bloke can really play a concertina,' mused Gently as he slammed his door.

Within the circle of light two grotesque figures were

111

hopping and gyrating. Ponderous, massive, yet with a sort of elfin agility, they gave the impression of something non-human, of mindless animals caught in a bewitched pattern.

'It's Ted Thatcher and Cheerful Annie doing a hornpipe, sir!'

On the roof of the wherry sat Pedro, Pedro the Fisherman. It was Pedro who was swinging and twirling the concertina. Never a false note trilled and cascaded from his long, tip-flattened forgers, never a pause interrupted the ecstatic rhythm. Like a Pied Piper of Upper Wrackstead he wove his spell and the corpulent couple had to obey him, though sweat trickled down their none-too-clean faces.

'Go it, Annie! Keep it up, Tedda bor!'

All around the boat-dwellers sat or squatted, clapping in time and shouting encouragement. Some visitors moored along the bank sat on their cabin roofs laughing and applauding. And there was no end to that lilting music. It frolicked on and on with rapturous and infinite variation. The very soul of music seemed to have settled in Pedro's concertina, seemed to be releasing itself through his runaway fingers.

Gently moved over to the magic circle of lamp-light.

'Cor . . . couldn't we half do with this bloke down at the "Chequers"!'

'Come an join us!' panted the dripping Thatcher, catching sight of Gently. 'Dew I can dance the Starmth Hornpipe, there i'nt no reason why yew shoont!'

But Gently was more interested in the slim figure perched on the wherry's cabin roof.

For a moment, as he regarded it, the curly hair, angelic eyes and shy smile faded into stolid East Anglian countenance beneath a peaked chauffeur's cap.

Then he shook his head and turned away.

'Come on, Dutt, we'd better ring HQ.'

'Just a moment, sir . . . it ain't often you get a basinful of this!'

Gently shrugged and went back to lock the car. As he pushed open the gate of the cottage he nearly ran into a thin, white-haired person who was standing there as motionless as the gate-post.

'Ah, Mrs Grey! I didn't see you in the dark.'

She made no reply. By the faint glimmer of light from the lamps he could dimly descry her set, ashen face. There were tears running silently down it.

'Mrs Grey . . . but what's the matter?'

She gave a little broken sob.

'They say they've seen him . . . my nephew.'

'Seen him! Seen him where?'

'Here . . . going into my cottage. But it i'nt true, Mr Gently. It i'nt true! They're a lot of good-for-nothings trying to make trouble for me! I woon't hide him . . . not though he's my own sister's boy!'

She broke down in a fit of sobbing.

In the distance, Gently could see Dutt throwing off his hat and joining in that seductive hornpipe.

113

CHAPTER NINE

HICKS HAD BEEN seen, but nobody knew who had seen him. That was the result of lengthy and exhaustive questioning.

About three in the afternoon the rumour began. Mrs Grey had set out to shop in the village at half-past two. Cheerful Annie was having a nap on her bunk. Ted Thatcher was fishing, Pedro gone off strawberry-picking and the rest of the community disposed in their various forms of idleness. And sometime during the half-hour that followed Joe Hicks was seen sneaking up the path to let himself into the cottage. By three o'clock, the knowledge was common property. Only everyone had heard it from somebody else.

By guile and sarcasm, Gently did his level best to break the vicious circle.

'There's only thirty-three of you . . . suppose you stand in a row, each one next to the person who told him!'

They were perfectly willing to try – if they could have remembered who in fact *had* told him.

'It can't be mass hysteria . . . do some of you know the difference between seeing a thing and being told it?'

But it wasn't any good. Nobody would own up. Fact or illusion, the image of Joe Hicks creeping into his aunt's cottage seemed to have drifted into the little community on a passing breeze: everyone knew, nobody had seen.

And Gently had other worries, anyway.

'The super's getting jumpy,' Hansom had told him on the phone. 'The Coroner's beefing about his inquest and he's a pal of the CC's. The super wants to know if we're going to make a grab in the next twenty-four hours . . .'

'Coroners . . .!' exploded Gently with deep feeling, as he hung up the phone.

In the morning things looked brighter. They had a tendency to do so over Mrs Grey's breakfast table. Also, Gently noticed once more, the mind had a way of sorting things out while one was asleep . . you went to bed with a problem and woke up with a new slant on it. Or a better attitude, which was sometimes as good.

'We goes into town, sir?' enquired Dutt, soaking up the last of the bacon-grease with a piece of bread.

'We goes into town, Dutt.'

'If you don't mind, sir, I reckon we might dig something up at the bus-station, the times of them buses being so cohincidental.'

'You're dead right, Dutt – that's your assignment.'

'Though I got to admit, sir, it beats me what the connection is there.'

Gently reached for the ginger marmalade and dredged up a tidy spoonful.

'You have to remember that we've got two camps at "Willow Street" – pro-Lammas and anti-Lammas.'

'Yessir. I see that, sir. But what business could Miss Pauline have with this Brent woman?'

'Well . . . this Brent woman might be running into trouble once Mrs L. found out about her. And she had found out, if we're to believe Mr Crow.'

Dutt nodded intelligently and rescued the marmalade.

'But how would Miss Pauline know where to meet her, sir?'

'She wouldn't, would she, unless she knew the whole plot.'

'Then why don't we just pick her up and spring it on her sudden, sir?'

'Because we've got nothing to spring, Dutt – not until we can prove she met Linda Brent.'

The sapient Dutt allowed that his senior had got something.

The super was out when Gently reported at HQ and Gently was duly thankful. Hansom's print men had done a sterling job of work at 'Willow Street', but the results were entirely negative. They had acquired good specimens of Lammas' prints and of Hicks'. It was Lammas' which were found on the reverse of the drawer that had contained the gun. And Mrs Lammas', of course . . . but they were accounted for. For the record Hansom had sweated out a press pic. of Lammas. It wasn't too good. One got the impression of a dapper, athletic-looking man of middle-stature, expensively dressed, a touch of distinction about a badly caught profile and iron-grey hair.

Gently said: 'You've had nothing in about Hicks?'

Hansom laughed a hard laugh.

'I'm having that photo circulated . . . what gives you the idea that Hicks has been financed and tucked away somewhere?'

'He's supposed to have been seen at Upper Wrackstead yesterday afternoon.'

'Seen?' – Hansom's mouth gaped open.

'Supposed to have been . . . it's probably just a rumour. I can't get hold of a first-hand witness. I ran over the cottage to please Mrs Grey and Dutt took a shufti at the boats. We didn't find anything.'

'But Jeez – shouldn't we get a man out there?'

'Maybe we should . . . though he'll show up like a sore thumb.'

Back in the Wolseley Gently sat for a minute or two gazing at the well-polished facia board. Then he solemnly produced and tossed a coin. It came down heads.

Pacey Road was a shabby-genteel thoroughfare off Thorne Road. It consisted of rows of late Victorian iced-cake houses, solid though stupid, and derived an air of sooty forlornness from the nearby marshalling yards of Thorne Station. Most of it had been taken over by the County Council and Gently, cruising slowly down, discovered the Drama Organizer's office at the extreme and stationmost end. He was lucky, they told him. One didn't often catch the Drama Organizer in his office.

Gently introduced himself and stated his business. John Playfair, an impish, smiling little man with bushy hair and glittering brown eyes, checked his information with scientific thoroughness. Yes, Pauline was one of his most promising young players. Yes, she had been waiting at the door of St Giles' Hall when he got there for rehearsal on Friday. What time she left he couldn't be sure . . . he was trying to iron out the Hovel scene, he seemed to remember. But it was round about her usual time. She had flashed him a goodnight and a promise to be there all day Sunday.

'Did she seem upset at all that evening?' Gently prompted.

'Well . . . there you are! I can't swear I noticed anything different about Pauline – I wasn't really on the look-out for it. As far as I was concerned, she was her usual cheery self.'

'Of course, you knew Mr Lammas pretty well.'

The smile died from the Drama Organizer's eyes.

'Yes . . . poor old Jimmy! He'd been the backbone of the Anesford since our St Julian's Hall days . . . it's a shocking thing to have happened to him.'

'Was he popular with the Players?'

'He was rather more than that . . . he was almost a tradition with us. Life won't be quite the same here with old Jimmy gone.'

'He wasn't in the present production, however?'

'No.' Playfair frowned. 'I wanted him to play Kent, but he said he couldn't manage this time. This is an extra production, you understand – we're putting it on for Festival Week. It isn't easy to get people at this time of the year.'

'Did he say why he couldn't play?'

'Well . . . something about business. One doesn't bully people, you know.'

'Had business ever stopped him before?'

'No. But then, we've never put on a show in July before.'

Gently half-lofted a shoulder in acknowledgement of the loyalty implicit in the other man's reply.

'He was a good actor . . . what sort of parts did he play?'

'Jimmy? He was a comedy actor . . . one of the best I've ever seen. The stage lost something when Jimmy went into business. The amateur stage, you know, is plagued with people who simply play themselves – the amateur who can create character is the rarest of rare birds. And Jimmy was that rare bird. Heaven knows how we're going to replace him!'

'He was very attached to his daughter, was he?'

'Very attached indeed.'

'You knew something about his family affairs?'

'A little . . . though not from Jimmy. It was Pauline who dropped something occasionally.'

Gently nodded and picked up his trilby.

'And his secretary . . . did he ever mention her?'

'No – never, within my hearing.'

'Thank you, Mr Playfair.' Gently extended his hand. 'If I should still be in town next week, I'll make a point of getting along to your Lear!'

The tails side of his coin took him to a thirties-looking reinforced concrete building which stood on the river

119

bank near Count Street bridge. Count Street was dull and industrialized, showing high, bleak walls diversified with an occasional small shop, or a flint church which had got lost during the nineteenth century. The warehouse of Lammas Wholesalers Ltd. was quite an adornment.

Gently turned in at the open gate and parked in the yard. Four steel-shuttered doors over a loading-ramp were closed and locked, but a smaller door at the side stood ajar. He pushed it open and went in. In the office to his right an elderly man in a dark suit was working at a high desk.

'Hullo . . . you the sole survivor?'

The elderly man turned to survey him through steel-rimmed spectacles.

'The Police again?' he enquired a little tetchily.

Gently grinned and admitted the fact.

'We can't help it . . . not when people get themselves killed! What's your name, by the way?'

He was Mr Page and he had been the head clerk. A shrivelled, martinet of a man. He hadn't the slightest right to be there nor the remotest prospect of being paid for what he was doing . . . but he was doing it all the same. He was tidying up the loose ends of the business.

Gently settled himself on a table and stuffed his pipe with Navy Cut. There was something incredibly dreary and posthumous about this place . . .

'You always been with Lammas?' he asked.

'I have. At least, ever since the firm was founded.'

'How long have you been head clerk?'

'Since the beginning of the war. Our last head clerk was a younger man. He volunteered for Army service.'

'You'd know everything that went on here.'

'In the line of business, certainly. That is what head clerks are for.'

'Well . . . what about this realization? Didn't you know about that?'

'It could hardly have been carried out without my knowledge.'

Lammas hadn't quite pulled the wool over Page's eyes, but he'd got pretty close to it. He'd built his story round the approaching termination of his lease on the warehouse. Because of that he was reducing stock, because of that he was selling off trucks and vans. And if it meant the loss of business? Page needn't worry his head about that! Lammas was conducting highly secret negotiations for the lease of bigger and better premises. When the firm acquired these it would blossom out on a scale it had never approached before. And then Page, of course, could expect a substantial augmentation of his salary . . . even an allotment of shares, to increase his interest in the firm.

Yes . . . Lammas had played it well enough to keep Page guessing, if not satisfied.

And after all, hadn't Page been witness to Lammas' business acumen all these long years?

'What about Miss Brent – you must have noticed something there?'

Page tightened his mummified lips.

'Miss Brent worked in the ante-room to Mr Lammas' office, which is across the corridor. It was not my business to spy on my employer's conduct.'

'But you'd got an idea?'

'I have seen nothing suspicious.'

'I'm not asking if you caught them *in flagrante delicto*, . . . just if their attitude struck you as suggestive.'

Page eyed him in hostile silence.

'Looking at it another way . . . if you *had* noticed something, would you have felt it your business to drop Mrs Lammas a hint?'

The ghost of a flush appeared in Page's corpse-like countenance.

'This . . . has to do with the case?'

'Oh yes! Very much it has to do with the case.'

'It is not my business, you understand, to be a passer of idle gossip.'

'I wouldn't be asking if I didn't require the facts.'

'Very well . . . since I have your assurance. I did in fact drop such a hint.'

'When!' rapped Gently, with such venom that Page nearly toppled off his stool.

'When . . . why . . . it was Friday morning! I rang her up when the wage cheque was refused . . . she drove into town directly with money to pay off the staff!'

It came out easily then. Page was suddenly rather frightened. He had gone to the bank at the end of the morning to cash the cheque and when it was refused, had started putting two and two together. Mrs Lammas, when she arrived, had put them together even faster. Where was Linda Brent? She hadn't been in that week! What was going on at the business? The unhappy Page had had to admit that it was practically sold out.

'Who else was present at this interview?' fired Gently.

122

'Nobody – they had gone to lunch!'

'And why didn't you tell the police about it?'

'I – I looked upon it as a private matter . . . Mrs Lammas advised me to keep it to myself . . .'

'How did you find out about the *Harrier?*'

'I didn't – I didn't know anything about it.'

'Then where did Mrs Lammas get her information?'

The head clerk wrung his hands anguishedly.

'She went into his office . . . she might have found something amongst his papers!'

With a snort Gently got up off his table and slammed across the corridor into Lammas' office. It was a neat, well-furnished room, looking out on the drab river-frontage. Gently sized it up quickly. There was a shallow document drawer at the top of the green steel desk. On the desk lay a slightly bent paper-knife and the drawer was bent and scratched above the lock. He whisked it open. No need to look further! The current Blake's List stared him in the face, turned back at the *Harrier*'s entry, and under it lay Old Man Sloley's confirmatory letter . . .

'Haven't you got any keys to this desk?'

The shattered head clerk had followed him into the room. He shook his head helplessly.

'Well . . . I doubt whether he would have left anything interesting, though we'll have to make sure.'

He ruffled through the other papers in the drawer, then threw them back impatiently.

'Look here! I'm pretty certain Lammas was up to something we don't know about. Why not make a clean breast? He's dead now and in any case he hasn't treated you any too well.'

'But there was absolutely nothing . . .!' Poor Page was almost ludicrous in his agitation.

'There must have been something! What were those mid-week trips of his about?'

'They were to negotiate the new property . . . that's what he told me!'

'And you believed it – you, with your finger on the pulse of everything going on here! Do you think we're imbeciles? You couldn't help having an idea. And don't think you'll be left here any longer to cook the books and cover up!'

This was too much for the head clerk. He drew himself up with a fury that almost startled Gently.

'Sir . . . *sir*! If you continue in these allegations I shall request the presence of my solicitor. I will *not* submit to such preposterous accusations!'

'All right . . . all right!' Gently waved him down pacifically. 'We'll check the books anyway . . . I'm only giving you a chance to come clean.'

'But I have nothing to admit, sir! I am here purely in the office of a caretaker – unpaid, I may say. My services are gratuitous—!'

'I'll believe you . . . don't labour it.'

'—doing nothing but answering correspondence, which, sir, must be done!'

Further protestations seemed to hover on the out-raged Page's lips, but he was interrupted by the sudden clangour of the dead man's phone. For a moment both of them stared at it, ringing away insistently on the corner of the desk. Then Gently grabbed it up and limbered it to his ear.

'Chief Inspector Gently.'

It was Hansom at the other end.

'I've been trying to get you for the last hour . . . thought you might like the latest bulletin from Upper Wrackstead.'

'Upper Wrackstead!' Gently stiffened. 'You don't mean you've picked up Hicks?'

'Not yet . . . not quite!' Hansom's voice sounded gloating. 'But we've picked up a specimen of the larky lad's handiwork. You remember that fat burglar's wife – Cheerful Annie, they call her? Well, they found her in the Dyke this morning . . . with a .22 bullet through her head!'

CHAPTER TEN

THE SUPER'S HUMBER decorated the scene of the crime when Gently arrived there. The great man was standing beside it holding forth to Hansom, while two plain-clothes men and the local Constable added dignity to the composition. In scared little groups the river-dwellers stood near their boats, even the children subdued and watching.

'I want him,' the super was delivering himself, 'and I'm going to *have* him! I'm going to have him if it means drafting in blasted military. Why man, nobody's life is safe while this damned chauffeur is at liberty – he's running amok, he'll put a bullet into anybody who recognizes him!'

'We've got the district cordoned,' put in Hansom defensively. 'There's road-blocks on all the main—'

'Road-blocks!' snapped the super, swinging his arms dramatically at the surrounding marsh and carrs. '*That's* where he is – not playing tag with your road-blocks! Get some men in there – get a lot of men in there. I don't care whether they sink in up to their backsides – I want

126

Hicks winkled out before he shoots down any more innocent bystanders!'

Hansom made a face outside the super's range of vision. He knew, if the super did not, what it was like beating an alder carr . . .

'Ah . . . and *you* Gently!' The super's eye fell on the Central Office man. 'Where were *you* when Hicks was blazing away last night? You're a Yard man, aren't you! You're one of those "lucky" types whom things creep up on! Well, there was something crept up here last night and I'll bet my last chance of promotion you were sleeping like a baby, forty yards from the spot! And that, after you'd been told Hicks was lurking around here!'

Gently heaved his bulky shoulders non-committally.

'That was only a rumour . . . we investigated it thoroughly.'

'Only a rumour! Only a rumour!!! And I suppose the body they've just carted off is only a rumour, too! I tell you it's not good enough, Gently. You might have prevented what happened last night. Ever since you've come down here you've been wasting your time probing and prying into the Lammas family, while the real criminal has been left running around loose . . . and now this happens, right under your very nose! If you'd exerted yourself in the right direction we might have pulled in Hicks before he had a chance to pot anyone else.'

Slowly Gently fumbled in his pocket for a peppermint cream and balanced it on his thumb.

'Why,' he asked simply, 'would Hicks come here?'

'I don't give two hoots why Hicks came here!'

'But it's a relevant question . . . this is the last place you'd expect to find him.'

The super looked as though he'd bite him. 'I don't care if it's so bloody irrelevant that Scotland Yard would lie down and weep! He's been here – he was seen here – and he's done another killing here. That's all that matters, and that's all that's going to matter. We didn't know where to start looking before, but we do now, and by glory we're going to have him sitting in a cell before he's very much older!'

Gently shook his head with the slightly admonishing air that superintendents took so hardly.

'We don't know he was here – we don't know that he was seen here. All we know is that the gun which killed Lammas killed Annie Packer . . . and we don't know that either unless we've recovered the bullet.'

And he skilfully popped the peppermint cream into his mouth.

'All right!' breathed the super chokingly. 'All right, Gently. Let's play it your way for half a minute. If it *wasn't* Hicks who shot Annie Packer, perhaps you can tell me who in high heaven else would want to do it?'

Gently nodded his approval. 'That's what one should ask one's self . . . though unfortunately the choice is rather wide. But I can suggest a motive, if you feel it might be interesting.'

'I do, Gently . . . it just happens that I *do*!'

'Well . . . it might occur to a clever sort of criminal that we weren't taking as much interest in Hicks as we might be and that a carefully prepared episode of this sort would remedy the situation. The likelihood would

128

be all the stronger if Hicks was only the fall-guy in the first instance . . . wouldn't it? And it wouldn't hurt him any if he was already making well-paid tracks for South America . . .'

The super stared at him evilly, but he was too good a policeman to brush an idea aside.

'You mean this rumour about Hicks being seen was a put-up job?'

'That's how it struck me . . . after I had investigated it.'

'In fact Hicks never was anything but a red herring – the door is still wide open?'

'Pretty wide open. Though it may have closed a little lately.'

The super brooded for a spell. 'It's narrow enough, if you ask me. If Hicks was just a blind then there's only two people in it – Mrs Lammas and her son Paul. Nobody else would get Hicks to play. I suppose you can add the Brent woman – he might have been infatuated with her. But it's pointing all the way to Paul and Mrs Lammas.'

'And maybe one other.'

The super glanced at him keenly.

'I keep getting the impression that we haven't got a full list yet . . .'

'Any reason for that?'

'Not really . . . just a place in the picture for him.'

'It's a "him" then and not a "her"?'

'Oh yes! I think it has to be a "him".'

The super brooded some more with a terrier-like glint in his eye. Then he said nastily:

'There's just one little flaw in this precious theory of yours, isn't there?'

'There may be several . . .'

'Yes – and the first one is how an outsider could spread a rumour about Hicks in a little closed community like this – without being identified! Did that cross the Central Office mind?'

'I admit . . . it rather puzzled me.'

'Ah! It rather puzzled you! Well, it isn't going to puzzle me, Gently. There's been too much puzzling in this case already. Now we're going to have some action – a lot of action! Hansom, get back in that car. We'll leave the chief inspector to do his puzzling while we tackle this thing like common, everyday policemen!'

There was a relaxed murmur amongst the river-dwellers as the super's Humber departed, as though the great man's presence had burdened their independent spirits. Gently, of course, was another matter . . . apart from being a resident he had a chameleon-like quality of blending with his environment. They crowded round him as though he were their personal representative with the latest news.

'What are they goin' to do, mister?'

'Why did Joe Hicks do for our Annie . . .?'

'They aren't goin' to make trouble, are th'?'

'Yew don't think that wa'nt none of us!'

Gently gazed at the nondescript group with a humorous wonderment.

'You – lot – of – baboons!' he exclaimed at last. 'Don't you realize you've brought this on yourselves? If you could have told me last night who spread that rumour about Hicks, Annie Packer would be with us now – and Dutt and myself the only coppers for miles! Why do you have to be so infernally dumb?'

They shuffled a bit and looked rather abashed. Ted Thatcher eased back his greasy cap and scratched beneath it.

'Now hold yew a minute, bor!'

'Yew can't remember evra mortal thing!'

'An we reckon we know now ennaway . . .'

'What was that?'

Gently turned to the last speaker, who chanced to be the slattern. She met his eye defensively.

'Well . . . don't it seem obvious? We're been talkin' it over b'tween us.'

'Tha's right,' put in Thatcher, 'I know she told *me*.'

'*Who* told you?'

'W'poor ole Anna.'

Intelligence dawned in Gently's eyes.

'Let's get this straight! Is this something you'll swear in the witness-box, or is it something you've dreamed up because Annie doesn't live here any more . . .?'

They murmured indefinitely. Thatcher was the only one who stood his ground. Annie had told him and he had questioned the slattern's son about it . . . whereupon the slattern thought she might've heard it from the kids after all.

Gently sighed and shook his head.

'But there weren't any strangers around yesterday afternoon – people who don't usually come here . . .?'

He went over to Annie's wherry. Four frightened little faces stared up at him out of the hatch.

131

'Who's looking after the kids?'

The slattern, it appeared, was seeing they were fed and was keeping an eye on them.

Inside the low, wide cabin it was close and redolent with boat-smell, paraffin, blankets and a subtle tincture of Deep River. On one of the berths lay the slim form of Pedro the Fisherman. His pale face was half-turned into a cushion and there were silent tears running down it. Gently touched him on the shoulder. He moaned and sat up dazedly.

'You – you slept here last night?'

The Italian's haunted eyes looked vacant, but he nodded as though he understood.

'With Mrs Packer – with Annie?'

Now he shook his head. 'In da . . . da forra-peak.'

'Tell me what happened.'

Tears welled up again as Pedro tried to find words.

'We finish da music . . . go to bed. Sometime I don't sleep . . . hear her get up, go 'way. I hear. Da sound . . . lika da bird, *pzzzzzt*! Nodding else . . . nodding at all . . . I go to sleep.'

'When was this, Pedro?'

'When . . . I dunno. One hour, two hour.'

'But there must have been a splash! Didn't you hear that?'

Pedro shook his head stupidly, then his face twisted and collapsed, and he sank back sobbing on the bunk.

Gently took a quick look round the cabin and went back on deck.

'Who was it found her?'

He was a sad-looking man answering to the name of

132

Dido Plum. He had just been setting out in his dinghy for the village. As he was passing Annie's wherry he had seen something white down amongst the weeds. He had prodded it with his oar . . .

'Show me where it was.'

Dido led him up to the bows of the wherry and pointed to a spot slightly ahead of them. If you had toppled off the bows you might have fallen right there . . . with a splash. And with a bullet through the head you ought to have left a little blood somewhere . . .

Gently frowned, and stooping, raised the hatch of the forepeak. Below him lay a disordered bunk. On a shelf opposite was Pedro's concertina, lying unlatched and sagging drunkenly, beside it a silly little posy of marsh-flowers stuck in a potted-meat jar. Gently dropped the hatch back expressionlessly.

'Who saw the body . . . what was she wearing at the time?'

She'd been wearing a night-gown, it appeared, and a knitted cardigan over it. And slippers, but one of them was still in the Dyke somewhere.

'What would she have got up for?'

There were guffaws and tittering, and glances at a sheepish-looking Ted Thatcher. He grinned at Gently and turned on the others in mock indignation.

'Don't know what yew're all lookin at me for! Ennaone'd think I made a habit of strange women.'

'Well don'tch'?' shouted someone and there was a ripple of laughter.

Gently said: 'You were dancing with her last night.'

'W'yes . . . but that i'nt the same as what this dirta-minded lot seem to think!'

'She could have arranged to see you later.'

Ted gave him a wink. 'Yew're nearla as bad as they are, an tha's pretta bad!'

'Did she, or didn't she?'

'She di'nt then – though I woon't say she ha'nt got a mind tew. But that wa'nt noth'n definite, an' I aren't agoin' to have m'reputation dragged in the mud!'

It was suddenly comedy, that tragic occurrence on the river-bank. Perhaps it was reaction, perhaps it was the East Anglian resentment at being thrown emotionally off balance. But the comic side had come uppermost and the river-dwellers wanted it to stay uppermost. They insisted in finding something superlatively funny in the idea of the dead woman creeping out to meet Thatcher.

'Were you expecting her?' persisted Gently.

'W'not exacla . . . but I woonta been surprised.'

'Did you stay awake, for instance?'

'What me – for that ole bitch!'

'Then you didn't hear anything – your boat is moored quite close?'

'That i'nt apurpose either – onla b'cause there i'nt no room with better compana!'

He had heard something, all the same. When Gently could steer him away from the gallery he admitted to having been awakened. He had then heard the same sound that Pedro described.

'Like an ole swan that was, or like a cute when she's

134

a-sittin' on some eggs. "Pssssh!" that go, onla a bit more wicious-like.'

'Didn't you get up to see what it was?'

'W'no . . . I'm tew far uppa the tooth to get up evra time I hear a funna noise.'

'And you've no idea of the time?'

'Blast yes – yew can see me strikin a light to have a look!'

Like Pedro, he had heard no splash, and like Pedro he had dropped off to sleep again. Two other witnesses, the slattern and a little man with a big moustache, contributed substantially similar evidence. The little man could add a trifle more he had stayed awake longer. Ten minutes or so after the hissing there had been a subdued bump, as though somebody had stepped cautiously into a dinghy, and there followed a number of similar noises occupying several minutes.

'But not a splash?'

'No, there wa'nt no splash.'

'And of course you don't know the time?'

'I don't – but I could hear "Moanin' Minnie", if tha's enna help to yew.'

'Moaning Minnie' was the automatic foghorn off the coast, ten miles distant. It had probably been booming all night.

Gently bit his lip and stared about him at the rough, worn grass of the river-bank. Why wasn't there any blood? Cheerful Annie had looked as though she had plenty!

He had got the tragedy into some sort of focus now. In his mind's eye he could see what had gone on here while he was sleeping so peacefully in the nearby bungalow.

It was twelve when he had gone to bed. Perhaps in deference to the resident coppers, the jollifications on the bank had ended half an hour earlier. A few people had stopped to chat, no doubt, but it hadn't continued very long. When Gently had doused his light and drawn his curtains it was quiet and still outside. After that, how long had it been? How long had Annie given Pedro in the forepeak to drop off, before she pulled on her cardigan, stuck her feet into her slippers and crept away to try her charms on Ted Thatcher? An hour, perhaps. It would have been around one. At one or just after she had slipped ashore, turned riverwards towards Thatcher's old tub and . . .

But that was where the picture went hazy. For the life of him, Gently couldn't fill in the next bit. If she'd been attacked between the wherry and Thatcher's boat, where was the blood? If she'd been enticed to a distance first, how could four people have heard the fizzing of that silenced .22 Beretta? And if, for some inscrutable reason, she had gone to the bows of the wherry . . . right above Pedro's head . . . and been cleanly bowled off into the Dyke, why no splash?

Once she was dead, the picture grew clear again – at least, the picture of what had happened: the motive wasn't quite so obvious. Her body had been lowered into a dinghy, the dinghy had been pushed out to the stream-side of the wherry and the body noiselessly jettisoned. So it wouldn't be found too quickly . . .? That was just possible. If that were the reason, then it

136

was necessary to jettison the body towards the middle of the Dyke, since it ran shallow near the bank.

But where was the blood . . . where was the blood?

Shaking his head, Gently explored the whole length of the bank, his eye fixed now on the grass, now on the decrepit collection of dinghies belonging to the various boats. The most suspect was Annie's own, moored between the wherry's bows and the bank. But like the others it showed nothing more sinister than certain years of undisturbed grime.

'Here, bor . . . dew yew come an have a look at this!'

It was Thatcher, who, quietly satisfying his curiosity about Annie's wherry, had poked his nose into a cardboard box he had found lying with other junk on the cabin-top.

'What is it . . . the crown jewels?'

'No . . . but it might blodda well buy a set!'

Gently stepped aboard and went over to him. The old sinner's eyes were almost staring out of his head. Packed in the box, and completely filling it, were ten crisp bundles of one-pound notes . . . bundles which an experienced eye would estimate at a hundred apiece. And on the lid of the box was written in sprawling block letters: For Annie's kids.

'Blast!' barked Thatcher. 'Cor rudda blast!'

And it was not, Gently felt, putting it too strongly.

They found him a sheet of brown-paper in which to wrap the box. The box itself was easily identified. It had been taken from the communal rubbish-heap and was a shoe-box which had been discarded by one of the river-dwellers. Thatcher watched him mournfully as he tied the package up.

'I 'spose them kids aren't never goin to see that again.'

Gently shrugged. 'If my guess is right this money has been stolen.

'But dew your guess is wrong, what happen to it then?'

'That's a nice point of law . . . I don't think I'm qualified to answer it.'

'That must be wunnerfiul to be a copper an turn up evidence like this here!'

Gently tucked the package under his arm and went down the wherry's plank. At the rubbish-heap he paused, measuring distances with his eye. Then he stooped and picked up something. It was a tiny tube wrapped in gold foil.

'Blast!' exclaimed the disgusted Thatcher. 'He's even pickin' gold sovereigns off our blodda rubbish dump!'

CHAPTER ELEVEN

A N EXUBERANT DUTT had ridden in with the first load of the super's search party. He found Gently picking at his lunch in Mrs Grey's parlour and wearing the wooden expression which told of much and significant ratiocination. In front of him on the table lay the little gold-wrapped tube, one end closed, one end ragged. It appeared to be filled with a darkish, greasy substance.

'Here we are, sir. How are things at your end?'

Gently grunted over a forkful of salad.

'I've bought a new corpse and been torn off a strip!'

'Yessir.' Dutt curbed his enthusiasm. 'I heard all about it up at H.Q., sir. Flippin' cheek it was, popping the old girl off right under our bedroom window. And why didn't we hear the shot, sir – that's what I can't make out!'

'A "Parker-Hale", Dutt.'

'You got the gun, sir?'

'No . . . but I've got four witnesses and they all describe the same thing.'

Dutt whistled softly. 'But how did he get hold of that, sir . . .?'

'I don't know, Dutt, unless he picked up one second-hand and screwed the barrel himself.'

'He'd need tools, sir.'

'There's a set of dies in the garage.'

'Then you reckon it *was* Hicks?'

'No, Dutt. It might have been anyone. Lammas might have fitted one himself without knowing he ought to have his licence endorsed.'

'All the same, sir . . . it doesn't half point towards the shover.'

Dutt brooded a few moments to show a proper respect for the problem, but he was obviously impatient to impart his own especial findings.

'Well sir, I takes a squint at the corpse on account of you hadn't seen it, but what I really has to tell you—'

'You've seen the corpse, Dutt?'

'Yessir. Bullet went clean through, forehead to top-back. But—'

'Anything strike you about the night-dress?'

'No sir, 'cept a bit might've been torn off the hem—'

'Ah!' The far-away look came into Gently's eye. 'I'd just got round to that angle when you came in . . .! Now just hold on a minute, Dutt – I'll be right back with you!'

And still clutching his fork, he dived out of the room.

Dutt sighed and cut himself a generous slice of pork-pie. There were times when his senior was a little less than appreciative.

The fork was still in Gently's hand when he returned

ten minutes later, but in his other hand he now held a sodden strip of rayon.

'There! Would that be the bit torn off the hem?'

'Yessir. Daresay it would. It's the same material.'

'Exactly, Dutt . . . and it answers a pressing question. He'd had the corpse in a dinghy at one stage and that corpse would have bled. But it wouldn't have bled with a bandage tied round its head . . . that's why I can't find any blood in the dinghies. At the same time, it must have bled somewhere before he bandaged it . . . and then again, why should he bother about the blood . . . ?'

'Yessir. Very true, sir.'

There was a plaintive note in Dutt's voice that succeeded in penetrating Gently's abstraction. He grinned at the sergeant's expression of injury.

'All right . . . let's have the story.'

'Ho, hit will wait, sir. I ham a bit peckish.'

'Go on, you old so-and-so!'

'Don't want to hinterrupt your cogitations . . .'

He thawed out, however, as he remembered the glowing details of his discoveries. Fortune had smiled on Dutt in his investigations at the bus station. At first it looked like being a frost. The conductor who had been on the six-twenty bus from Halford remembered nobody of Linda Brent's description, neither did an inspector who had got on down the road. Dutt had persisted with odd members of the station staff who might have seen the passengers leave the bus, but he got precious little encouragement until he chanced to see a Wrackstead bus pull in. And there he struck oil. Because the romantic young conductor cherished a secret passion for Pauline Lammas and her unexpected presence on the six-fifteen on Friday lingered sweetly in his memory.

'Saw the whole thing, he did!' related Dutt excitedly. 'Couldn't want a better witness, sir. When they comes in after a run they goes and gets their money and tickets checked in a glass-fronted booth affair, and Miss Pauline, she goes and stands in the bay right next door. Of course, this charlie keeps his mince-pies on her, and being as how there was a couple of blokes ahead of him, he's still there when the Halford bus gets in. And sure enough there's a fancy dark piece gets off it with her baggage. Up goes Miss Pauline and helps her off with her things, then she fishes in her bag and hands something over.

'And this is the juicy bit, sir – he saw what it was! 'It was a Yale-type key on a ring with a white tag.'

'A Yale-type key . . .!' Dutt had the pleasure of at last seeing his senior sit up and take notice. 'And what does that suggest, Dutt?'

'Well sir – after giving the matter me best attention–'

'Go on, Dutt.'

'It occurs to me, sir, that Mr Lammas couldn't have had any hideaway like Hinspector Hansom was led to believe.'

'You mean that otherwise there would have been no need for Linda Brent to collect a key from Miss Lammas.'

'Well, would she, sir? Mr Lammas would've give it to her himself. But no – she has to pick it up! So we deduces that the key wasn't available when Mr Lammas sets out on the preceding Saturday, but was so on the Friday. And from that we further deduces that it's the key to a rented property, and that Miss Pauline knows where Miss Brent is at this living minute!'

Gently nodded soberly. 'And we also deduces something else – that wherever Lammas went on his mid-week trips, it wasn't to prepare and furnish a hideaway.'

Dutt wriggled impatiently 'She might know a whole lot else, sir!'

'She might, Dutt, and she might not. Don't forget that she's on her father's side in this. If she knew enough to put the finger on someone there's no reason to suppose she wouldn't do it . . . even if it were someone in the family.'

'But she must know all about what Mr Lammas was going to do, sir. If we crack into her now she may come across, and then if we can pick up Miss Brent . . .'

'Perhaps, Dutt, perhaps. Did your platform Romeo notice what happened to Miss Lammas and Miss Brent after the key was passed?'

'Yessir, in a manner of speaking. They goes off down the station to where there's three or four buses parked and Miss Lammas sees Miss Brent into one of them.'

'You checked where they were going?'

'Of course, sir, automatic. One was going to Cheapham, one to Summerton and one to Sea Weston.'

'Cheapham and Sea Weston!' Gently stared in surprise. 'That's a fascinating set of buses, Dutt . . .! But it gives us two to one on the coast. If I were a betting man I'd take odds on Linda Brent being tucked away in a seaside bungalow, wouldn't you?'

'Yessir. Now, do we pull in Miss Pauline . . .?'

Gently considered at length over the strawberries he was dipping in sugar. All the time his eyes were fixed on that diminutive foil-wrapped tube.

'No,' he said at last. 'No, I don't think we'll trouble Miss Pauline at the present juncture.'

'But if we can find Miss Brent—!'

'That's a job for you.'

'For me, sir?' goggled Dutt.

'Yes – you're specializing in this angle! Go back into town and beat around the estate-agents. Try the ones near Lammas' office for a start and then work outwards. Names won't be important, but dates and people will. You're looking for a rented furnished property, probably in the Summerton-Sea Weston area, let as from Friday, key picked up by a certain young female . . . say Friday lunch-time. It's mere routine, Dutt.'

Dutt groaned and rolled his eyes pitifully.

'Also, you can take this stuff in for checking . . .' Gently waved to the tube, his package and the strip of rayon, '. . . me, I feel a poetic mood coming on.'

'You feel a *whatter*, sir?'

'A poetic mood, Dutt. I feel it's time that Mr Paul and myself got down to a session of mutual illumination.'

The drowsy brilliance of the hot June afternoon seemed made to display the charm of 'Willow Street'. White walls under crisp reed thatch, ebony columns of timber, lattice-windows open wide, it nestled like a rare bird on

144

the dipping slope as Gently swung out of the rhododen-drons and braked to a stop. Around it the willows hung, completely still. The air itself seemed trembled to a stillness. Only a swallow-tail butterfly sailed, regal and self-assured, to disturb the spellbound sun-hush.

The gardener appeared from somewhere, roused by the sound of the car pulling up. He was a cadaverous, elderly man clad in a collarless twill shirt, black waistcoat and grey Derby trousers. Gently nodded and he came over.

'Anybody at home?'

'W'yes – no . . . I don't rightla know.'

He turned about to peer into the open garage, which was empty except for an expensive-looking motor-cycle.

'Daresay the missus have gone to Narshter – tha's her day for it. Miss Pauline, I can't answer for. Mr Paul, he's fishin' in the broad, dew yew want him.'

'Whereabouts in the broad?'

'W'now, how should I know that? Yew'll ha' to go an see.'

'Can I borrow a boat?'

'There's plenta in the boot-house.'

Gently shrugged and locked the Wolseley, but as the gardener turned away he asked:

'You weren't here last night, I suppose?'

'Ah. I was pickin black currants an' one thing another.'

'Did you notice anyone go out?'

'I hear Mr Paul go off, tha's all.'

'What time would that be?'

'W' . . . about eight o'clock time.'

'And when did he come back?'

'Not while I was here, an that was nigh on ten.'

The house was so silent as Gently went by that it might have stood empty for a century. Every window was open, every door ajar. He could hear an alarm clock ticking as he passed below the kitchen. Rounding the corner, however, he nearly tripped over the lumpish-faced maid. She was lying in the sun with her skirt pulled back, and jumped up indignantly at Gently's sudden appearance.

'I neffer did – and what are we to be expecting next, I should like to know!'

'Don't let me disturb your siesta!' Gently forced back an impish grin.

'Come into people's private gardens – sneak up on them from behind—!'

'I'm only going to borrow a boat. There's no need for you to get up.'

The maid shook herself like an outraged hen and followed him into the boat-house. It was a big, gloomy place, lit only from the entrance, and extending under at least half of the building above. It smelled sweetly of naked timber and floating oil. In the basin surrounded by a splined platform lay a husky-looking teak launch, one of the local Class half-deckers, a National, a pair of skiffs and a dinghy. Gently selected the dinghy and stepped into it with the confidence of one not unfamiliar with the habits of small boats.

'What time did Mr Paul get in last night?'

The maid pouted at him defiantly.

146

'I suppose he did get in before you went to bed . . .?'

'Oh yes he did, Mr Nosey, and not so late either, it was.'

'What excuse did he give for going out again?'

'Who said he went out again, after I took him his malted milk in bed, too!'

Gently pulled loose the painter and pushed himself out of the boat-house with a scull.

The broad at this end had an air of exclusiveness contributed to by a number of rush and reed islands. These not only served as a screen but also deterred the near approach of the thronging holiday-craft. In the secret waterways between them flourished superb water-lilies, while there was an air of tameness about the population of coots, water-hens and great-crested grebes. Gently surveyed these fastnesses with a jaundiced eye. He was suddenly struck with the size of the task of finding one particular human being, even on a medium size broad.

But the luck of good detectives was with him. Paul Lammas had not ventured far on that blazing afternoon. Two hundred yards from the boat-house Gently perceived the bows of a dinghy sticking out past a tangle of rushes. Rowing a little nearer, he could see a fishing-rod and the tip of a stationary float. A little nearer still and Paul came into view. He was lying on cushions in the back of the dinghy, head cradled in his arms, staring into the blue of the sky. Gently let his own boat glide silently in and bump against the other.

'That's a fine way to catch fish!'

Paul started forward out of whatever dream he was in.

147

'You . . .!'

There was something terribly feminine about his delicate features and fine, soft hair. Today he was wearing a fawn linen shirt and grey-green slacks, his jacket lying rolled in the bows. Feminine . . . but with a difference.

'Why have you come here looking for me?'

Gently shipped his sculls without replying and grabbed himself a handful of reeds around which to loop his painter. Paul watched him fiercely.

'I wanted to be alone . . . surely that was clear enough?'

'They told me you were fishing.'

'I am – and I want to fish alone!'

Gently grinned and settled himself with his pipe.

'There isn't any bait on that hook, for a start . . . mind if I have a look? Then again, if you got on the shady side of these reeds . . .'

'What is it you want – you haven't come here to teach me how to fish!'

Gently nodded and applied himself to Paul's rod and tackle. He was probably fishing too shallow – the float could go up a bit! And one caught precious little with a piece of weed for bait.

Paul was sitting up straight now. He was staring at Gently with an expression of mingled anger and apprehension.

'If you think I've got anything to tell you, then you're very much mistaken!'

'What's in that tin . . . maggots?'

'I tell you you're wasting your time!'

'Let's try a cast over here, where there's a bit of shade.'

Furious, Paul bit his small mouth together and sat watching while Gently made a cast. Now he'd got that rod in his hand, the man from the Central Office seemed to be forgetting him entirely.

'Look . . . I knew that was the place to try.'

The float was shuddering excitedly.

'Now – there it goes. And it isn't a little one! Here, you'd better land it . . . I've just remembered I haven't got a licence!'

Paul snatched the rod out of his hand and played the fish in. It was a handsome sharp-headed bream, clean-looking and full of jump. With considerable expertise the young man slipped a landing-net under it, lifted it aboard and disengaged the hook. Then he threw it straight back into the water and put the rod well out of Gently's reach.

'Now . . .! Perhaps we can learn what Scotland Yard is here about.'

Gently extended his hands. 'First things first! Where did you go on your motorbike last night?'

'I went for a ride.'

'A ride – not *again*?'

Paul looked at him in surprise. 'What do you mean – not *again*? Is there any reason why I shouldn't?'

'Not really . . .! Where did you go?'

'To Starmouth. *And* I can prove it.'

'What time did you get back?'

'About eleven, I believe.'

'And you spent the night in bed?'

'Has it broken a local bye-law?'

Gently brooded a moment over his pipe, then his mild glance sought Paul's.

'Look! I've pretty well made my mind up about this business – but not quite. There's a whole lot of features that keep getting in the way, and I've got to know which of them belong and which of them don't. And I think you could tell me – if you stopped looking on all authority as your natural enemy!'

The young man's flush sprang burning in his cheek.

'I've told you before—'

'Yes, I know what you've told me before. But things have moved on a bit since then – enquiries don't stand still, you understand. And what you told me isn't good enough any longer . . . that's what it amounts to.'

Now he looked hard at Paul.

'We don't have to be enemies, remember.'

There was a silence between them broken only by the puffing of Gently's pipe and the jewelled twitter of a reed-warbler somewhere close at hand. Fifty yards away a pair of grebes watched them suspiciously, swimming flat and jerky on the water. Then there was the slightest of chuckles and the grebes had vanished.

'You mean I'm not under suspicion?'

Gently's head barely moved to indicate the negative.

'It was absurd all along – you *couldn't* have thought that I did it!'

'But you've made a bad impression.'

'I don't care. I'm just not the type!'

It was true, and in more ways than one. Gently tried to conjure up the picture of the frail young man manoeuvring the enormous remains of Cheerful Annie.

'And if I'm not under suspicion, why can't you just leave me alone?'

'I've told you . . . because you've got some important information.'

'And I say I haven't, so what are you going to do about it?'

'First, I'm going to tell you just where your mother stands in this business.'

There was no doubt about it being a shock. Paul's cheek was a barometer to his emotions that a child could read. But Gently was in no hurry to press home his advantage; he puffed contemplatively for a while, his eyes dwelling dreamily on the golden-shadowed stars of the water-lilies.

'You know . . . your mother fits the bill rather neatly.'

Paul's teeth were almost chattering and he had to fight to keep a countenance.

'I ask you . . . as one intelligent person to another . . . don't you think your mother would be capable of homicide as a last resort?'

Now he had to put his hand on the counter to steady himself.

'As I read her character it is completely implacable. She has a psychopathic will-power, a destructive will-power. I feel reasonably certain that she would sooner destroy a person than relinquish her hold on him.'

'No!' gasped Paul. 'You don't understand – she's had to stand up for herself, that's all. She isn't what you say!'

151

Gently shrugged. 'You should know . . .! But to me, as an outsider, that's the picture. And we have there the motive. Her husband is trying to escape. *You've* got a motive too, but yours isn't nearly as strong . . . neither, as you will remember pointing out, are you the type!'

Paul choked, his eyes fixed wildly on the Central Office man.

'Of course, at first we couldn't show that your mother knew anything about Linda Brent or your father's plans to disappear. That made your mother's position reasonably safe. We might suspect it, but we couldn't show it, and it's only the things you can show that impress a jury. But now, I'm afraid, we can show it too.

'By lunch-time on Friday your mother had all the relevant facts but one.'

'But she didn't – she *couldn't* have known!'

'Your father's whereabouts? No – not at lunch-time! But she took steps to discover it . . . another point for the jury. And then there's the matter of the fingerprints on the drawer which contained the gun – her's of course, superimposed on your father's – and her lies about her movements – it's a pretty formidable list!'

Paul's state was truly pitiable. His shaking made the dinghy vibrate till it produced fine, shivering lines on the glassy surface.

'She wouldn't have shot him . . . she didn't know anything about the gun!'

'What do you have to know about a double-action automatic, except to point it and pull the trigger?'

'She'd have to load it . . . she couldn't do that.'

'Wouldn't it be loaded, when it was kept handy to deal with burglars?'

'But she couldn't . . . I tell you she *couldn't*!'

Gently hunched a shoulder, as though it didn't matter either way.

'That won't be the charge, in any case. We know who pulled the trigger. The charge your mother will face in dock will be conspiracy to murder, and if you think Hicks will shield her, you haven't followed many cases of this sort! And incidentally, we've got Hicks nicely netted. He's probably under arrest by now.'

'Stop!' croaked Paul, scarcely able to speak.

'I thought you should know the situation.'

'It isn't true . . . you've got to listen!'

'On the facts, we shall have to make a charge.'

'No . . . listen to me . . . only listen! I'll tell you all that happened on Friday!'

Gently turned to look at him, sitting shrunken and crouched in the stern of the dinghy.

'Ah!' he murmured. 'I was hoping that you would.'

The story that Paul told was as pathetic as its narrator. He hadn't known a thing about his father's projected disappearance until the quarrel late at night. For him, the tragedy had been on quite a different key. Even now he seemed unable to get the matter out.

'You see . . . she met him at a party.'

His mother had a lover.

'His name is Henry Marsh . . . he's a solicitor in Norchester. Heaven knows what she sees in him! I could tell him for a cad at a glance.'

But his mother had fallen for him, and he for her. There had been a head-over-heels romance lasting three months and during that time Paul's heart had accounted for quite a number of weeks' absence from the university.

'When did all this happen?'

'She met him at Christmas . . . it was going on till Easter.'

'Did they keep it under cover?'

'I suppose so . . . anyway, *I* knew about it!'

'What about your father?'

Paul shrugged feebly. 'I couldn't say what *he* knew.'

From the beginning Paul had been suspicious and before long he had had a row with his mother. It was then he was made to realize that he had slipped into second place. His mother wouldn't listen to him. His old influence with her had vanished. For the first time in his life he felt the icy wind of neglect seek out his pampered ego and after astonishment and self-pity had run their course he reacted in strict character.

'At first I threatened to commit suicide, but she wasn't impressed by that. Then I told her I would inform Father unless she stopped seeing him. It was this that put an end to it – for the moment.'

It would, of course. Mrs Lammas had no intention of either losing or being lost by her husband. A love affair was all very well while it remained a gay flourish to the pattern of life. It was not very well when it threatened to disrupt that pattern, to demolish reputations, to liberate a bondman. So Mrs Lammas had yielded, or at least appeared to yield. When Paul was around she no longer drove off to her discrete rendezvous.

Gently wondered what sort of certificate Paul would get from his mother's specialist the next time National Service reared its ugly head.

'But you weren't satisfied?'

'No . . . I knew the difference in her manner towards me! Once we were everything to each other, nothing could come between us. Now she was cool, so horridly cool! How can I describe it? She no longer confided in me and I felt I could no longer confide in her. All the little things that pass between people who love one another! And I knew I couldn't trust her. She had put me outside her heart. I was sure she would tell me the biggest lie without a grain of remorse.'

So it had become an armed peace between mother and son. Outwardly, everything was the same. Inwardly, they spied upon each other, two enemies, each watching to catch the other at a disadvantage. And Paul couldn't be away from Cambridge all the time.

'That's the real reason why you are at home, is it?'

'Of course it is! You knew what I told you was an excuse. While I was here she had to stop seeing him . . . before this happened, anyway. If she went out, I followed her. What else was there I *could* do . . .?'

On the Friday morning he had followed her into Norchester and witnessed her visit to the office. During the afternoon she was very silent and absorbed in thought. At about half-past three he had passed through the hall and found her in the act of telephoning. She had immediately hung up and avoided him by going into the kitchen and giving some orders about tea. A little later he had seen her slip out of the house by the kitchen door.

'She went to the phone-box at Wrackstead Turn. I timed her. She was talking for twenty minutes.'

Suspicious and very much on his guard, Paul had laid his plans for the evening. Instead of staying in the house he would deliberately go off on his motorcycle and then lurk in a side-turning, waiting to see what she would do. Mrs Lammas fell into the trap. Within five minutes she had set out to visit her lover. On the way, for motives then obscure to Paul, she had turned off to Halford Quay and made some inquiries of a petrol-pump attendant. But then she went directly to Marsh's house. She had remained there for the rest of the evening.

'You're sure of this – it's important, you know!'

'How can I be other than sure, when I was watching the whole time on a thousand knives! She drove straight up the drive as though she owned the place, parked the car so it was out of sight and ran into the house without even knocking. Do you think I took my eyes off it one second after that?'

Gently nodded, satisfied. If Paul were telling the truth, no plain-clothes man could have watched that house half as intently as the slighted spoiled boy . . .

'I watched for nearly two hours, from just after half-past seven till just before half past nine. Then she came out, and him with her – patting her shoulder and all that sort of slush! When she got into the car I raced back home. I wanted it to be a surprise, didn't I just! And I waited for her in the lounge – and that was the row the servants heard.'

Under the circumstances, he had simply refused to believe her excuse that she had gone to Marsh for advice. What sort of tale was she telling him, about his father having sold out the business and gone off with Linda Brent? It was all too ridiculous! A palpable invention! They had gone on rowing till the return of Pauline put an end to it.

Gently refilled his pipe and lit it meticulously.

'All right . . . it hangs together. Now where is Henry Marsh's house?'

Paul hesitated before replying. He had talked himself back into fettle.

'I suppose you've got to know?'

'Oh yes, I'm afraid we have.'

'Very well, then – and please don't think it's something significant! – his house is at Ollby.'

'His house is *where*?' The spent match stayed put in Gently's fingers.

'At Ollby, about quarter of a mile from the turning. But I can tell you right now that it means exactly nothing!'

It seemed an age before that spent match was flicked into the water. Gently kept staring at it as though it were something he hadn't seen before. Then it went suddenly, with a curve of irritability, and Gently was lugging out his beginning-to-be-dog-eared Ordnance Survey.

'Come on, now! No fooling about. Just whereabouts is that house situated?'

Paul pouted at his rough tone, but pointed to the spot.

'Yes – just where I thought! It's that white house with the trees round it, standing all on its own . . . over a mile this way from the village, and a good two from Panxford Upper Street!'

'But it doesn't signify – it might have been twenty miles away!'

Gently's eyes fastened on him and there was no mildness in them now.

'You can't be that stupid! Don't you realize what you've told me? On your own admission you, your mother and this Marsh were within half a mile of the scene of the murder at the time it was going on.'

'That's just the point – I can *prove* she didn't go there!'

'On the contrary, Mr Lammas . . . you can't even prove that *you* didn't go there.'

The cheeks blanched to their incredible whiteness, as though Gently had stabbed him with a knife. Even the hand clutching at the counter was drained of colour.

'You – you trapped me into telling you this!'

Gently shook his head. 'You seem to have trapped yourself.'

'I told you in good faith – now you're making it evidence against me!'

'You told me because you had to tell me something . . . how much remains to be seen.'

'I told you everything!'

'Then look at this map.'

He prodded at the buff coloured line of the secondary road taping out from Wrackstead. It left Panxford to one side, passed through the hamlet of Panxford Upper Street and for over three miles from thence to Ollby proceeded without a single side-turn . . . except one.

'You must have seen the chauffeur pass.'

158

'I didn't, I tell you!'

'You must have done, if you were on that road. Do you want me to believe he went ten miles about?'

'I wasn't watching the cars!'

'You'd have noticed your father's.'

'I'd got my back to the road!'

'Then you'd be in full view of the house.'

Paul swayed as though he would fall and Gently halted to give him time to recover.

'Another thing . . . you'd have seen the smoke.'

Paul moaned like a stricken animal.

'From the house the trees hid it, but you'd have seen it from the road.'

'I didn't see anything.'

'Then you must have been blind!'

'I'm not going to say any more . . . I told you the truth, and now you're trying to trap me!'

He sank back into the cushions and threw his arm over his face. Gently bit hard on his pipe-stem, looking down on the crumpled form.

'You see where this is leading – it could have been you and the chauffeur. There's nothing to show you didn't intercept him and persuade him to help kill your father.'

Silence; except the twittering of the reed-warbler.

'You were pals, weren't you? If it comes to that, you might even have made the phone-call.'

Silence, complete and utter.

Gently snorted and reached for the painter. 'Very well, then – for the present! But you're in dangerous waters, my lad, and you'd better do some hard thinking.

It may be that only the whole truth will save you from a long drop – and be a close call into the bargain!'

He pushed the dinghy clear. Once more the reed-warbler began to twitter from its world of tall stems.

CHAPTER TWELVE

PHYSICALLY THE WOLSELEY was an oven, spiritually it was an ice-box. You could almost feel the waves of refrigerating hate coming from the angry woman in the rear. Upright she sat, like a tiny princess. Her dark, flashing eyes tried to drill holes in Gently's unexpressive back.

'I still don't understand, inspector!'

'I regret the necessity, ma'am.'

'I have already been into Norchester once this afternoon. If you had anything to ask me, it could surely be asked at "Willow Street"!'

'We require your presence, ma'am.'

'I shall certainly consult my solicitor!'

The briefest of ironic smiles flitted across Gently's homely features as he pulled out to slide past a truck. He had been on the phone at 'Willow Street' before Mrs Lammas got back.

But the smile didn't last. He was quite frankly a bit out of his depth. The more he delved into this case, the more perplexing it seemed to get. The more you found out, the less did it add up into a coherent and satisfying whole . . . as though each new piece in the jigsaw threw the others just a little out of true.

But they were all legitimate pieces – they had to fit into it somewhere!

And yet . . .

He banged on his horn and shook a wandering cyclist.

Well, you went on asking questions, and let the theory take care of itself.

The city was buzzing with the news of Cheerful Annie's demise and the resultant manhunt. It leapt from the fly-sheets and made banner heads across both locals and Londons.

MANHUNT FOR MAD KILLER – link-up with Broads slaying, ran one of the latter. Body Taken From Dyke – Police Searching Marshes, said the more conservative *Eastern Evening Star*.

Gently pulled over to a news-stand and bought a sheaf. No mention of .22 bullets . . . the Londons were guessing. 'The Police are still eager to contact the chauffeur, Joseph Hicks, missing since the discovery of the remains of James William Lammas in a burnt-out yacht a few miles from the scene of last night's tragedy. They believe he could assist them in their inquiries.' A question of two and two!

'Here . . . you may not have seen this.'

He handed the papers back to his icy passenger.

'Another reason why we specially want you at Headquarters.'

She wouldn't even bother to make a comment.

Hansom was waiting on the steps, looking badgered and ready to bite someone. But he cheered up at the sight of Mrs Lammas ... wasn't he free, white and forty-one? A quick glance passed between him and Gently.

'This way, ma'am ... we shan't keep you waiting.'

He led her down the corridor and opened the door of an interrogation-room. Gently hung back and waited till the door was safely closed again.

'You managed to pick him up?'

'Yeah – but not without some agony.'

'Never mind, as long as you've got him. Are there any results on that stuff I sent in?'

'The rayon fits for sure – it came off the night-dress.'

'But what about the rest?'

'Someone has been very clever! There's nothing on the tube – it'd been out in the weather. The shoe-box was weathered too. It had a nice set of your prints and a dirty smudge on the lid.'

'That'd be Thatcher's paw! But what about the notes?'

Hansom laughed nastily. 'That's where someone was clever. First of all they'd replaced the paper bands with rubber bands – you probably noticed that. Then they'd removed the top and bottom note from each bundle, making ninety-eight to a bundle instead of a hundred. Result, a clean bill of health. We can't even trace the clerk who paid them over the counter.'

Gently nodded ponderingly. 'Sounds a bit too intelligent for the average run in chauffeurs.'

'That's what I thought, but of course you never know.'

'This romp on the marsh . . . has it flushed anything yet?'

'Not a blasted sausage and the super's as peeved as hell.'

'Well . . . here's an outside tip. I don't promise it will pay off. Take a search warrant and two or three men and see what you can find at "High Meadow", Ollby – that's Marsh's place. I'd put your men out back, by the way . . . there's a plantation sheltering the house which might have been put there to fade into.'

'You mean that house near the turn?' stared Hansom.

'Yes, and give the servants a once-over. I'm particularly interested to know what happened there on Friday evening.'

'You darned-well bet I will!'

'And ring through here.'

Hansom departed at great pace, the gleam of the hunter in his eye. Gently stood still a moment, gazing after the vanishing form. Then he sighed very softly to himself and turned the handle of the interrogation room door.

The Headquarters of the Norchester City Police was a modern building, completed shortly before the Second World War. Outside it was a well-flavoured and handsome pile in Portland brick and stone. Inside it bore an unhappy resemblance to a requisitioned morgue and the interrogation room was no exception to the prevailing climate. It was bleak and inherently depressing. The steel desk, steel chairs and steel filing-cabinets did nothing to relieve the gloom. Once you set foot in here, they seemed to say, you were as good as lost . . . you might just as well confess to something and have done. Mere innocence was stripped off you at the doorway.

The room, however, seemed to have made little impression on Mrs Lammas. It was doubtful whether she had even noticed it. She had appropriated the desk with her handbag and gloves, lit a cigarette and now stood glowering at nothing, in the centre of the floor.

'Won't you sit down, ma'am?'

Disdainfully she perched herself on the edge of the nearest chair. It seemed positively gigantic in relation to her. Gently glanced at the rather-superior chair behind the desk, but decided not. He sat down on the desk itself.

'To begin with, I want you to know that this interview is informal.'

She breathed scathing smoke at him. Her cigarette was coloured and slightly perfumed.

'What you may tell me now won't be used as evidence unless you give your permission. It's between you and me, without any witnesses.'

'Thank you. But I am well aware of what is evidence and what is not.'

'Then that point's settled! Now — would you like to do the talking?'

'Talking? What about?'

'Why . . . about your movements on Friday.'

She stared at him without emotion. The cigarette hung like a pink ornament between two exquisite fingers.

'Be good enough to explain! You are no longer satisfied with my statement?'

'Not really, Mrs Lammas. That's why I'm giving you this opportunity.'

'An opportunity, indeed!'

'Yes . . . to explain certain facts.'

'What precious facts are they?'

'Some rather serious ones which have come to my notice.'

She stubbed out the cigarette. It was only half-smoked. In the stuffy atmosphere the scented fumes lingered in a faint miasma.

'You will kindly tell me the facts.'

He nodded without looking at her. 'I'll tell you what I can prove . . . perhaps you'd like to go on from there. In the first place you had a call about the bad cheque from your husband's head clerk. You went to the office. You discovered what your husband was up to. You discovered about Linda Brent and the trip on the *Harrier*. You told the head clerk to keep quiet about your having been there. And in the evening you went looking for your husband and making inquiries as to his whereabouts.'

'That's all you can *prove*?' Her question came like a whip-crack.

'Yes . . . just for the moment. Though there are a few subsidiary points – like your fingerprints being on the drawer that contained the gun.'

'That is readily explainable.'

'I know. But it's still evidence.'

'I am prepared to admit everything you have found out.'

'It would be hard to do otherwise.'

166

'Nor do I agree with you that it is particularly serious – I am quite certain that you wouldn't venture to base a charge upon it.'

'Is that to be your answer?'

'Do you really expect any other?'

'I think it's reasonable to expect you to bring your statement up to date . . . since you're admitting that it's substantially untrue.'

Mrs Lammas reached for her bag and took out a fresh cigarette. A jewelled lighter no larger than a walnut clicked and flamed. This time the cigarette was blue . . . its aroma was subtly different, Gently noticed.

'It's the evening you want to know about, isn't it?' she breathed.

'Naturally . . .'

'If I was looking for my husband, then I might conceivably have found my husband – and put him out of the way.'

'As you say . . . conceivably.'

'But that isn't what you think.' There was scorn in her tone. 'You're the sort of fool who'd warn me, according to the rules. You're too sentimental to be a good policeman, Chief Inspector Gently.'

'It's the good policeman who sticks by the rules . . . but we won't go into that! Where did you go from Halford?'

'Is that where I admitted I went?'

'The petrol-pump attendant recognized you.'

'Then I certainly wouldn't bother to deny it.'

She paused deliberately to puff and exhale, her brown eyes examining him with unfeigned calculation.

'Where do *you* say I went, inspector – even though you can't prove it? You said our conversation was to be informal.'

'I'm not sure of my evidence . . . that's why I'm asking. But it might impress a jury more than it does me.'

'How very intriguing! Then it would make up your charge for you?'

'It might form the basis of one, unless I hear something different.'

'And I won't tell you different, will I, because I'm not impressed with your secret evidence. We seem to have reached an impasse, inspector – or shall we say you are being a little clumsy?'

Gently looked at her woodenly. She was feeling well on top now! It wasn't even worth being angry with him when she could lead him on so adroitly. And she knew where she stood, this diamond-sharp little woman – she wasn't to be frightened by talk of charges or long faces!

'We're not getting far.'

He grunted and got off the desk.

'We aren't, really, are we?'

'No . . . so it's time we had some help!'

Dramatically he strode across the room and threw open the dividing door. A tall, dark-haired man sitting on a chair immediately opposite quickly looked up. And for the second time in two days Gently's ears rang to the blood-curdling shrill of Mrs Lammas' scream.

'This is completely illegal!'

Henry Marsh was trying to establish his dignity, while Mrs Lammas clung whimpering to his arm.

'You had no right to bring me here to play this trick on Mrs Lammas!'

He was a good-looking man, though his grey eyes ran a little close. He had a large, straight nose, a broad, curving jaw, a sharp chin and small, neat ears. He wore a clipped moustache and a lot of long hair brushed straight back.

'I shall consider whether it is actionable – I assure you there will be some very unpleasant repercussions!'

Gently shrugged and took his seat, this time behind the steel desk.

'There are other things which have unpleasant repercussions, Mr Marsh . . . withholding evidence is one of them, especially for gentlemen in your profession.'

'Withholding evidence! What do you mean by that?'

'I mean that certain information has been received concerning yourself and Mrs Lammas and the events of Friday night . . . information which, in the light of the interlude you are at present acting, I believe to be correct.'

'Sir . . . I warn you to be careful!'

'I assure you, Mr Marsh, that I shall be *most* careful.'

'You are dealing with a solicitor now!'

'The point had not escaped my notice.'

Marsh glanced down at Mrs Lammas as though he would rather have liked to free himself from her handicapping grapple, but she was much too firmly ensconced. He resigned himself to a part of injured nobility. Gently stubbed the bell-push on the desk.

'I take it you will make a statement?'

'I could refuse, sir, without the slightest prejudice.'

169

'Naturally, I shall divulge the extent of my information.'

'You can scarcely expect a statement unless you do.'

Mrs Lammas moaned faintly and disengaged her head from Marsh's waistcoat.

'Let me tell him, Henry . . . I'm the only one he cares about.'

'No, Phyllis! You must say nothing further unless I advise it.'

'He's a devil, Henry . . . for God's sake let me get it over with!'

'We are not obliged to tell him anything except in explanation of this alleged information.'

There was a tap at the door and there entered a shorthand Constable and a plain-clothes man. They took up their positions obsequiously, although the plain-clothes man indulged in a hard, police-issue stare with its faint overtones of penal servitude. Mrs Lammas suddenly separated herself from her protector and went back to her chair. Marsh hitched up his trousers, looked round and took a seat nearer to the desk.

'Your full name and address?'

Marsh rattled off particulars without the slightest need of prompting.

'Now . . . the information is this. You, Henry George Marsh, have, since about Christmas of last year, enjoyed an intimate relationship with Phyllis Thais Lammas. Would you like to comment on that before I go any further?'

Marsh shook his head briefly and Gently continued:

'On Friday, June 23rd, Phyllis Lammas went to her husband's place of business in Norchester and there learned that he had realized his assets, that he had hired the yacht *Harrier* from June 17th till June 24th, that he was on terms suggesting intimacy with his secretary Linda Brent, and that Linda Brent had been absent from the office since she left it on June 17th midday. Following this discovery Phyllis Lammas made a telephone call of twenty minutes, which she attempted to conceal. It is suggested that she made the call to you.'

Gently paused again, and again Marsh confined himself to a shake of the head. Mrs Lammas, however, gave a little start and her small mouth shaped the word 'Paul!' Marsh made a gesture to her.

'On Friday evening Phyllis Lammas drove from her home at "Willow Street", Wrackstead to Halford Quay, where she made inquiries after the whereabouts of the yacht *Harrier*, her husband and Linda Brent. She then drove to your private house, "High Meadows", at Ollby. She was alleged to be there from just after half-past seven till just before half-past nine p.m. I will not have to remind you that during that time her husband, James William Lammas, was shot and killed at a distance of not more than half a mile from "High Meadows" and an attempt made to dispose of his body.

'This is my information as it affects you . . . I think you will see the necessity of giving a complete and accurate statement of all that took place that evening.'

Marsh took his time. He was clearly not a person to be rattled. With his fingertips placed together he had listened intently to what was said and now he was examining it, testing it and adding up its implications.

A tough nut he'd be for a prosecution to crack.

At last he was ready. One hand clenched and struck firmly into the other.

'As regards the first part of your information, I do not propose to make a statement.'

Gently nodded. He hadn't really expected one.

'Mrs Lammas stands to me in the relation of a client to her solicitor. That is all I have to say about *that*. But with regard to the remainder, I am not so unreasonable as to offer no explanation, though I have no intention of going further than what you say seems to require.

'It will be unfortunate, Mr Marsh, if you withold anything material.'

'I shall use my discretion, sir, as to what I consider material.'

Gently shrugged and made a gesture. It wasn't everyone who took the trouble to warn you.

'I have said that Mrs Lammas stands to me in the relation of a client to her solicitor. It was therefore not unnatural that she should contact me after learning that her husband had illegally realized the capital of the firm of Lammas Wholesalers, Limited, in which, you will be pleased to remember, she is a shareholder, though a small one. She had also to discuss the consequences of his apparent disappearance in the company of his secretary.'

'Excuse me, Mr Marsh . . . but was it so natural to discuss these matters on the telephone?'

'I was merely given the heads, sir—'

'Wouldn't she have called in, or made an appointment?'

'Certainly. And an appointment was made.'

'And that was the whole substance of a twenty-minute call?'

Marsh hesitated, but it was only the hesitation of a master-fencer who discretely withdraws from an awkward position.

'There was, of course, subsidiary matter . . . we are all human, all liable to emotion in time of stress. I do not think the subsidiary matter is relevant to the present purpose.'

'You were not surprised, then, that she didn't straight away call on you at your office . . . it isn't far from her husband's . . . directly she made this distressing discovery? Or for that matter that she didn't straight away phone?'

Marsh hesitated again, but still on perfect balance.

'That is something my client must answer. I have no doubt she will. I have no doubt that when you put the question to her she will tell you that at the time of the discovery she was completely stunned and unable to think out a coherent course of action. I would not be surprised to hear my client give such an answer to such a question.'

Gently nodded admiringly. 'Thank you, Mr Marsh. I must remember to ask her! Would you continue your statement?'

Marsh rubbed his hands as though rinsing from them the previous issue.

'My client's problem was pressing and required immediate attention. Unfortunately I was engaged at the time she called me, which would be at about 4 p.m., so I consented to see her in the evening at my residence. This is an unusual but not an unprecedented occurrence. A lawyer, like a doctor, must be prepared to see his clients at irregular hours. The appointment, as you have been informed, was for half-past seven and for approximately the next two hours Mrs Lammas and myself were engaged in a consultation, details of which will not concern you. She apprised me, however, of the inquiries she had made at Halford. She had undertaken them to confirm, if possible, what she had learned in the morning. With reference to the frightful tragedy taking place across the marshes, we neither knew of it nor saw anything to report. For this reason I advised my client, when the fact became known, to say nothing of a visit to a spot in such close proximity to the scene of the crime, a circumstance which must lay her open to quite unwarranted suspicion and interference.

'This, sir, is the extent to which I have withheld evidence or caused it to be withheld. I think you must agree that I have transgressed neither against the law nor against the code of my profession, and that it was as unnecessary as unworthy to play this trick of yours on my respectable and bereaved client, Mrs James William Lammas.'

It was well done, and he knew it was well done. He placed his fingertips together again and sat back a little in his chair. Gently grunted and twisted a spill of paper he had been working up. A good story, even if it did leave out a few of the facts!

'This place of yours . . . "High Meadows" . . . it's quite a substantial property, isn't it?'

'A desirable small residence. I suppose you could call it that.'

'Six or eight bedrooms, perhaps . . . I've only seen it from the road.'

'There are eight bedrooms, if you wish to be precise.'

'You'd need one or two domestics, eh?'

Marsh saw it coming, but he couldn't prevent it. He did the next best thing and took it by the horns.

'There are three who live in, but they cannot confirm my statement. They happened to be out on the evening in question.'

Gently's eyebrows lifted. 'You mean all three together?'

'Yes. I had given them tickets for a show in Norchester.'

It was smoothly said, but there was anxiety underneath it. Gently was watching the hands grow white above the knuckles.

'When did you give them the tickets, Mr Marsh?'

'At tea-time, I believe.'

'That was after you had spoken with Mrs Lammas on the phone — after you had returned from the office, in fact?'

'It was, but I had planned the treat earlier.'

'You mean that they were looking forward to it?'

'No . . . I kept it for a surprise.'

'Then in view of Mrs Lammas' appointment you could easily have cancelled it?'

Marsh shifted his expensive brogues. 'I'm afraid it was out of my mind . . . when I had given them the tickets,

I realized that I ought not to have done. But you will be kind enough to remember that I was not expecting police investigation. It was not likely to become known that Mrs Lammas visited me when I was alone.'

'It has become known now, Mr Marsh, and I am not quite happy about the details. What show was this your servants went to?'

'It was a musical entertainment ... *The King's Rhapsody* was the title. I really must protest at this irrelevant cross-examination!'

'At "The Theatre Royal"?'

'Yes, at "The Theatre Royal".'

'When did you obtain the three tickets?'

'I picked them up on my way from the office.'

'You mean in the afternoon, after you had spoken to Mrs Lammas on the phone?'

'Naturally ... but I had booked the seats by phone earlier.'

'How much earlier – was it in the morning?'

'No ... I think not.'

'It was during the afternoon, then?'

'Yes, it would have been the afternoon.'

'But before you had your talk with Mrs Lammas?'

'I ... cannot exactly remember.'

'Then it was after you had your talk with Mrs Lammas?'

'I have said I cannot exactly remember! My mind was greatly taken up with matters of business ... no doubt I utilized some spare moments, but when it is impossible to say.'

'This is *humiliating*!'

Mrs Lammas had risen to her feet.

'Henry, I will not permit you to be harried and questioned like this on my behalf!'

There was emotion in her face now.

'Don't you see that he's *going* to know these things, in spite of you, in spite of me? How do you know what he's got up his sleeve! He'll have already checked with "The Theatre Royal" booking-office and heaven knows where else – he just sits there playing with us, knowing it all – ready to pounce on the slightest evasion!'

'Phyllis . . .!' Marsh put out a restraining hand.

'I don't care, Henry! I hate it. I hate them. The police are filthy, filthy, filthy! How can we call this a civilization when we have dirty people like this living amongst us – people who can tyrannize and dictate and make us submit to their sadistic prying? Tell them what they want to know! Tell them, and let us be rid of them! I've felt sick ever since I set foot in this place and if I don't get out soon, I *shall* be sick!'

Even Marsh didn't know what to say in the silence that followed. An outburst like this was not envisaged by the rules of the game.

Gently twisted his spill round a stubby finger.

'Of course, our sadistic spying relates to two sadistic civilian murders . . .'

'You are worse than they! A hangman is the moral inferior of a murderer!'

'But a murderer is no great shakes . . .'

'At least he has the courage of his crime!'

Marsh cleared his throat. His impressive features seemed to have grown tighter, gaunter.

'Phyllis, you really must control yourself and let me handle this matter. You are making a great mistake to allow this man to unsettle you.'

'I *will* speak, Henry! I can't keep silent any longer.'

'You are giving him a quite gratuitous advantage.'

'I don't care any more. I just want to get out of this beastly place!'

'Please remember that you may involve another person.'

'He could not be more involved than he is at present.'

'I cannot agree with you—'

'I'm sorry, Henry. I've had as much as I can stand.'

She came to the front of the desk and stood there, her head and shoulders barely rising above it. Marsh's hands were tightly clasped together. His eyes were fixed on her appealingly.

'Please instruct your man to take this down, Chief Inspector Gently.'

'I think I ought to warn you that it may be used as evidence.'

'Use it for what you like – but for heaven's sake take it down!'

Gently nodded to the shorthand Constable, who had got rather put out by the preceding exchanges.

'You want to know if Henry and me are lovers. Very well – we are! We have been in love since Christmas, as your informant very accurately told you. I take it that it was Paul? My son discovered this and threatened me. He threatened to tell my husband, unless the affair was terminated. If my husband had come to know of it he would undoubtedly have divorced me – so there is your

178

motive, inspector! I had not the slightest intention of being divorced.

'I have admitted going to the office on Friday and to discovering how matters stood. I now admit to the telephone call, in which I arranged to meet Henry in the evening, if I could shake off Paul. The call was not made from the office owing to the presence of the head clerk and I didn't go to see Henry because I knew Paul was following me about. In the evening I was foolish enough to believe I had got rid of him, so I set out in my Rover. Before I went I spoke to Hicks. I instructed him to let me know immediately if my husband got in touch with him . . . my husband had just bought a new Daimler and I thought it unlikely that he would leave it behind.'

'Just a moment, please!' Gently was leaning forward. 'What else did you tell Hicks . . . he was a confidential servant, wasn't he?'

'I told him what I thought necessary. Hicks is very loyal and discreet.'

'Did you tell him what had happened at the business?'

'I wanted him to understand the seriousness of the affair.'

'What I'm getting at, Mrs Lammas, is whether or not he knew that your husband might have a large sum of money in his possession.'

'I didn't tell him so, but I suppose he could have deduced it from what I did tell him.'

'Thank you, Mrs Lammas . . . please continue your statement.'

'Before going to Ollby I went to Halford Quay. It

had occurred to me that if my husband were returning with the *Harrier* he would be in the neighbourhood of Halford Quay. As you have taken such pains to find out, I did get news of him, and this confirmed what I had discovered at the office. So I continued to "High Meadows" . . . you were quite correct in assuming that Henry got rid of the servants on purpose.

'I arrived there at twenty minutes to eight. We discussed the situation and what I was to do. Shortly before nine o'clock—'

Marsh was on his feet. There was a tinge of pallor in his hitherto ruddy complexion.

'Phyllis, I protest! What you are going to say is positively suicidal!'

She turned to him coldly. 'I am going to tell him *all*, Henry.'

'But this is unnecessary . . . there is no need for them to know it! I beg you to stop a moment and consider the implications!'

'Mr Marsh . . . you will kindly sit down.' Gently's voice sounded stony.

'Sir, I have a right to consult with my client!'

'But not to hinder a witness.'

'She is about to incriminate both of us wilfully!'

'It will rest on her evidence – sit down, sir, or I must have you removed.'

The plain-clothes sergeant half-rose to give colour to the warning and Marsh sank back, almost involuntarily, into his chair.

'Go on, Mrs Lammas.'

Marsh groaned and held a hand to his face.

'I was saying that shortly before nine o'clock we were a little alarmed to hear a car approaching the house. Henry peeped out and saw that it was my husband's Daimler with Hicks at the wheel. He had come to tell me that my husband had rung for him, and that he was just going to pick up Mr Lammas and his luggage from the yacht, which was moored at the head of Ollby Dyke.'

'He told you where the yacht was?'

'I have just said that he did.'

'But when you knew that, wouldn't you have gone down to the yacht with Hicks with the purpose of frustrating your husband's plan to disappear?'

'God help you, Phyllis!' exclaimed Marsh. 'I tried to warn you what you would let yourself in for!'

Mrs Lammas shrugged impatiently. 'It is reasonably plain why I did *not*! In the first place, I began to doubt whether my husband really intended more than an illicit week with his mistress. I had never expected him to do more than ask Hicks to leave the Daimler at a garage for him. In the second place, he could not be out of my sight while he was with Hicks. Hicks would have kept me constantly informed of his movements.'

Gently nodded imperceptibly.

'Did Hicks know where they were going?'

'No. He had not been told.'

'He wouldn't have mentioned meeting Paul outside?' Mrs Lammas bit her lip.

'I knew nothing of Paul's escapade until I got home!'

'Then that was really all that happened?'

'Yes. Now you know about everything.'

Gently looked at her ponderingly, and then at the despairing Marsh.

'I wonder,' he said, 'I wonder, Mrs Lammas . . .!'

The telephone rang. It was Hansom reporting nothing from 'High Meadows'. Almost as soon as Gently laid it down it rang again, and this time it was Dutt.

'I got it, sir . . . it's in the bag! I found the place at the fifteenth flipping time of asking!'

'What's the address, Dutt?'

'Beach Lane, Summerton, sir. It's a summer bungalow, like what you said.'

'Well . . . get along over! We'll go and have a breath of sea air.'

'Yessir. Right away, sir. Be with you in just ten minutes.'

Gently hooked on the phone again and sat staring at the desk in front of him. Then he turned to Mrs Lammas and Marsh.

'Righto, then. That's all for today! I won't say I'm satisfied, because it'd be a long way from the truth. You'll be good enough not to leave the district. I say this without prejudice, Mr Marsh! I'd like you to hold yourself ready for further questioning.'

Mrs Lammas picked up her bag and gloves. She beckoned to Marsh with a frosty smile.

'Why bother to conceal anything now?'

He tried to smile back at her.

'It's bound to be in the papers – we may as well make the best of it.'

Somehow, Marsh couldn't echo the buoyancy of his client.

CHAPTER THIRTEEN

'I GOT A FEELING we're near the end of the trail, sir!'

Gently grinned at his colleague's enthusiasm.

'I wish I had that feeling . . . but this case keeps making a fool of me.'

They had had tea in the canteen at Headquarters and were now bowling along in the Wolseley under the unquenchable sun of late afternoon. Right through the Broads ran the road. It crossed three rivers, skirted two broads and opened up on either hand, huge vistas of mysterious marshland. Sails pocked and pointed the blue-gold embroidery. The towers of forgotten windmills stood out like castles of Faery. It was a strange land, a poetic land, a land burgeoning with fable and supernatural story.

And, as a matter of fact, the fishing was good wherever you chanced to drop a line . . .

'You say this bungalow was only taken for three weeks, Dutt?'

'That's right, sir. Booked by phone on April 5th.'

'Then he was only planning to stay there till the dust died down.'

'Or p'raps it was the best he could do, sir. April hisn't exactly early for booking holiday accommodation.'

They could see the marram hills now. Silver among the green, they peaked and undulated like a tiny range of mountains closing in the horizontal country. Beyond them fretted the invisible North Sea, lazy, treacherous. Before today it had found its way through those grass-whispering ramparts.

'It's no good, Dutt – I can't get a grip on the thing!'

He'd never been so far with a case without an intuition.

'There's four of them in it and it might be either one. Or all four together – or several combinations! I suppose we'll wind up hanging that chauffeur, if we can ever lay hands on him.'

'You thought to bring a gun, sir?'

Dutt obviously had a theory of his own.

'Yes – I brought one! Here, you might as well take it. But if you think we're going to raise Hicks . . .' He shrugged. 'I suppose we might at that. I'm getting to where nothing would surprise me.'

'If he ain't hopped it he's *here*, sir,' Dutt retorted doggedly, 'and since we *know* he ain't hopped it, well, here he must *be*.'

Gently sighed to himself and slowed down to take a turning.

The village showed up, dark, sun-dried brick clustered round a lofty flint-faced tower, nestling in the lee of the marrams. There was scarcely a tree that threw shade. Those that did were scant and dragged backwards

184

by the eternal east wind. Beleaguered by stony fields and sandy heath, Summerton fronted one like an island fortress.

'Where would Beach Lane be?'

'Keep yew right on, bor, an yew 'on't miss it.'

They threaded the twisted village street and came out beyond. An unsurfaced track meandered over the last two hundred yards to the marrams. There it sprawled off left, getting rougher at every yard, and three shanty bungalows lay scattered like dropped toys.

'Hssh, sir! This last one is it!'

Gently parked the car at some distance.

From the far side of the hills they could hear the dull rumble of breakers mingled with the screams of children, but from the three bungalows came neither sound nor movement. Some towels lay drying in the sun, a bathing-cap hung from a nail.

'Everyone's on the beach.'

They went in through a tumbledown gate. It was a poor, neglected little place, obviously put up for letting. Both doors were invitingly ajar and it took not more than fifty seconds to ascertain that three small rooms and a kitchenette were empty. Gently opened the only wardrobe. Two dresses and a costume! And the underwear in the plywood drawers was very strictly feminine.

'So much for Hicks, Dutt! And look here, in the sink – one cup, one saucer, one plate and one knife.'

'I just can't understand it, sir,' said the crestfallen Dutt. 'I've been working it out, sir, and I could've sworn we'd nab him here—!'

'It's that kind of case, Dutt. It's got a down on theory.'

185

'But facts is flaming facts, sir!'

'I know they are . . . only you've got to have all of them. Now put that gun away and let's see if we can pick up the coy Miss Brent.'

But the coy Miss Brent did not need picking up. She appeared at that moment, coming over the sand-hills. Beautiful and aloof, a striped beach-wrap over her ruched bikini, she swung herself gracefully over the soft-sand track. Then her eyes fell on the two men. She froze into instant immobility. Like a vision of Aphrodite, the coy Miss Brent stood framed in the June sea-sky.

'You are Miss Linda Brent?'

Gently had no doubt. Even behind sunglasses the heart-shaped face and straight black hair were the counterpart of the photograph he had never ceased to carry. And anyway . . . no, there could be no doubt!

'Yes . . . I am Miss Brent.'

Her voice was pitched high.

'We are police officers, Miss Brent . . . we are investigating the death of your late employer, Mr James Lammas.'

'Oh, I see.'

'And we think that you can help us.'

The age-old phrases! Gently had watched their effect on so many people at one time or another. But here there was fear, mortal, stultifying fear, as though he had announced a present execution. She could scarcely get down off the sand-hill.

'You had better get dressed, Miss Brent.'

'Of course . . . yes . . . I understand.'

'We shall require you to accompany us to Police Headquarters at Norchester.'

'Naturally . . . I understand.'

But did she understand, as she stood there trembling like a leaf? Her eyes seemed fixed on the sordid little bungalow, as though that alone was real in a world turned to horror.

'Perhaps you'd better pack a few things.'

'Yes.'

Only part of her was answering.

'We may have to detain you. You had better come prepared for that.'

She moved forward mechanically, as though he had touched a button. The beach-wrap had half fallen from her shoulder, but she made no effort to replace it. Dutt nodded to his superior.

'*She* knows what went on!'

Gently shrugged and felt for his pipe. He couldn't quite place it, that paralytic fear. She must have all the answers. She'd got an alibi that would stand up. The most they could pin on her so far was obstruction. Or . . . was it?

He glanced up sharply at the bungalow.

'If she'd pinched the money . . . *that* would take some explaining!'

'She knows about the rest, too, sir,' retorted Dutt positively.

'But the money would tie her in – there's nothing else to be so scared about.'

'She knows, sir, she just *does*! You can see it writ up all over her.'

'Then we're back with her and the chauffeur.'

'We always was, sir, 'cording to the way I reckon.'

Gently frowned in the evening sunlight. Why did nothing ever fit together in this confounded case? But Dutt was right, as far as that went. Guilty knowledge was written all over her. Once more you had to ditch a theory and accept a hard, unwelcome fact.

'Come on . . . let's take this bungalow apart. If the money's here we might as well find it.'

Excepting the bedroom, they took it apart. The poor little place was singularly unadapted for concealing secrets. Even the floor, that historic receptacle for caches, was rendered innocuous by the building being raised on piles, while an Elsan in the closet ruled out another favourite hiding-place.

'It's the bedroom or nothing!'

Gently snorted his disappointment. He didn't *want* Linda Brent scared like that – it was making hay of any intuitive feeling he might have had about the case. Unconsciously he had been ruling her out. Unconsciously, he had accepted a certain pattern that didn't require her as a principal. And now the wretched woman insisted on obtruding herself in his calculations – making bad worse, and the perplexing baffling.

He pounded ferociously on the warped panel of the bedroom door.

'Miss Brent! Have you dressed yet?'

Miss Brent did not reply.

'Miss Brent – be good enough to answer!'

A faint whispering sound was all that could be heard. Struck with sudden apprehension, Gently seized and rattled the handle. The door was bolted. He wasted no more time. The bulkiest shoulder in the Central Office crashed through the flimsy woodwork and sent the door reeling inwards.

'Gawd!' exclaimed Dutt, 'she's been and gorn and done it!'

On the floor, her head against a portable-gas fire, her beach-wrap draped over both, lay Miss Brent. And the gas fire was unmistakably turned on.

They carted her outside. She wasn't dead. A bout or two of artificial respiration brought her round, shuddering and moaning. She kept her eyes tight closed, but tears were streaming down her cheeks. Her mouth worked continually in sobs that didn't come.

'Why didn't you let me die . . . why didn't you . . . why didn't you . . .!'

'You must try to pull yourself together, Miss Brent.'

'I want to die . . . why didn't you let me die!'

'You have behaved rather foolishly. There's no need for this sort of thing.'

'I don't want to be hung . . . why didn't you let me die!'

Dutt saw the tired expression that came over Gently's face.

'Shall I run down and phone for an ambulance, sir?'

'Yes, Dutt . . . she'll have to have a check-up.'

'And a man to keep an eye on this place?'

'Yes, I suppose so.'

They carried her back into the bungalow and Dutt went off in the Wolseley. She lay quite still on a couch, tucked up in a couple of blankets. Gently went into the kitchen. 'A mild stimulant', the textbook said. He filled up the kettle and brewed a pot of the stimulant in question.

'Here . . . do you think you can manage this?'

She put out a shaking, automatic hand.

'You shouldn't have done this, you know . . . it isn't going to help you.'

She sipped the tea without replying, almost as though what he said didn't register. Her eyes were still glazed with tears. Her lips twisted and trembled over the edge of the cup.

'At the worst, it was worthwhile to see it through.'

Now she was looking at him.

'There's a lot you wouldn't have to answer for. That's absolutely certain! Whatever the rest is, you don't have to throw in the sponge yet.'

Big, staring eyes looking at him from a frenzied inner world, a lonely world, a hopeless world. Eyes which saw nothing but horror.

'Tell me!'

The words seemed to be spoken for her.

'*Have you got him?*'

It was hard to believe she knew what she was saying.

'Who?' whispered Gently. 'Who is it you're referring to?'

In some way there was a shift of expression in the very depths of those haunting eyes. A shutter closed somewhere. He had lost a momentary contact with her naked confidence.

'*You don't know!*'

A sort of ethereal triumph was welling up.

'*You don't know, and I shall never tell you!*'

'Miss Brent!' Gently cursed himself for the slip he had made. 'Miss Brent . . . it is in your vital interest to tell us all you know!'

She wasn't listening.

'Unless you cooperate, you will be in a very serious position.'

A fey smile shone through her tears like hectic storm sunshine.

'It doesn't matter now. You may hang me, if you like. *I shall never, never tell you!*'

'Please consider what you are saying.'

'*You may hang me, if you like!*'

It was too late. He had let her know what she wanted. There was a positive radiance in the beautiful, tear-flooded face. And as she saw him about to frame another question her lips tightened and she feebly shook her head.

He didn't know – and she wasn't going to tell him!

Gently covered quite a lot of ground up and down that meagre lounge during the half-hour it took the ambulance to arrive. Never had a case seemed such an unholy mess to him. There was so much that was coherent, if you shut it up in airtight compartments. But once you took it as a whole . . . Then it stopped being coherent. Then it became like a job-lot of pieces out of several different puzzles, with odd bits everywhere that wouldn't fit at all. Yet there was a governing principle somewhere. There had to be! However square the facts looked, one knew that at a certain moment on Friday evening they formed a complete and unbroken circle.

What wasn't he seeing, in all that hotch-potch of motive and opportunity? What was the dynamic factor that he kept passing over, time and again?

Right at the beginning he had had a hunch that something obvious was staring him in the face. It was time now he saw it! Hadn't he got all the facts?

'There's only the shover to pick up now, sir,' Dutt reminded him soothingly. 'We must get him soon – it only stands to reason.'

Gently grunted without conviction. Somehow, the chauffeur had never impressed him as being more than a cipher in the business.

'He's got the worst motive of the lot of them. He *may* have guessed that Lammas had some money on him!'

But that was no reason. As often as not it wasn't the motive that made the murder. People kill for the most pitiful of motives, often so petty and obscure that one could hardly believe in them. Lammas had once checked Hicks and that was quite enough for motive. It could rankle for years until it found an opportune moment.

'Anyway, this is too clever. There's intelligence and character behind what went on here.'

Such intelligence as Marsh had, for example. Or Paul. Or Mrs Lammas. Or all three in conjunction . . . what sort of murdering conference had taken place at 'High Meadows' that evening, while the 'loyal and discreet' Hicks stood by, the perfect tool, the perfect fall-guy? Marsh, to gain a rich bride! Mrs Lammas, to foil an escaping husband! Paul, to lay for ever the spectre of National Service and an honest job! It was just a happy coincidence that killing Lammas would be pleasant work for Hicks also.

But then there was this damned woman here, somehow up to her neck in it. Gently cast a none-too-friendly glance at the still, apparently sleeping form on the couch. In what possible capacity could *she* have been of the faction? And which was the 'him' she was carrying the torch for? Not Marsh, that was certain. It rested with Hicks and Paul. And Paul was the one you were compelled to cast for the part. And if she knew it was Paul, then Paul must have communicated with her . . . it was the only way she could possibly know.

Gently came to a full stop in his restless pacing.

They hadn't found any letters . . . but Paul had been out on his motorcycle yesterday!

'Stay here – I'll be back in a moment.'

He went striding out of the bungalow.

Next door a family party had just returned from the beach. They were a middle-aged couple with three young children and they were spreading out towels and costumes, and shaking the sand out of their shoes.

'Just a minute! I'd like a word with you.'

They all looked round at him.

'I'm a police officer making certain investigations . . . you may be able to help me.'

After some moments of suspicion, they were almost over-helpful. No detail was so trifling, but one or other of them could add it to the tally. Yes, they could remember Miss Brent arriving at the bungalow on the Friday. It was just after little Ernie had cut his foot on a piece of glass, by deduction just after 8 p.m. and he ought to have been in bed . . . oh yes, she was quite alone and carrying two cases, she was, and wearing one of those posh dresses and etc., etc.

'She hasn't left the bungalow since she came?'

No, of that they were certain. They had palled-up at once. She hadn't any side, though she did speak la-di-da. They had even had meals together and gone shopping in the village . . . the kids were quite attached to her, she'd put some plaster on little Ernie's foot and bought them all ice-creams.

'She wouldn't have had any visitors?'

No, she'd always seemed rather lonely.

'Yesterday evening, for example?'

It was quite impossible, since they had all gone to a travelling film show in the village hall together.

'One more question . . . it's about the mail. Does the post office deliver up here?'

It did. It came in the mornings. Every morning they had a letter from their daughter Marge, who they'd left at home.

'And Miss Brent has had letters?'

Miss Brent had had none. She had looked out for the postman, but no letter had ever arrived.

Gently left them to shake out their sandals.

Had the luck of good detectives forsaken him?

On the other side of the sand-hills the children's cries and booming combers sounded mocking beneath the sun.

There was sadness in the mien of Superintendent Walker, a brooding, angry sadness born of hunches that hadn't paid off. This was the second time it had happened and it was damaging to his morale. On the first occasion Gently had been unofficial, which had been a sort of excuse for disregarding him. But on this occasion he had come with full credentials and there was no excuse of any kind. Success, success alone, would have justified the strong man of the City Police in shoving Gently aside. And success, alas, had not come his way in any measurable degree. After a day of hard marsh-frisking, cordons and road-blocks, he was still a Hicks-less super. He had even begun to despair of ever laying hands on that elusive customer. And for this he had said harsh words, for this he had ridden the high-horse, for this he had risked the rap on the knuckles he would undoubtedly get from a Gently-fancying Chief Constable.

'Come in!'

It was Hansom, looking apprehensive at the rasping tone of the summons.

'He'll be in in a moment . . . just parking his car.'

'Is the Brent woman with him?'

'Nope . . . they carted her off to the Northshire and Norchester.'

The super drummed viciously on his desk-top.

'Well, he nearly let *her* slip through his fingers, didn't he!'

But there was no latent triumph in Gently's face as he and Dutt came into the office. Rather it was an absent-minded expression . . . he hadn't been saying a word during the drive into town.

'Sit down – make yourself at home!'

The super's sarcasm was intended to warn and give notice.

'You know what luck I've had – I don't need to tell you. There's just one small item that my ham-fisted methods have brought to light, and which wouldn't have turned up in any other way – that's it, on the chair.'

He pointed to a dark garment and a peaked cap of similar colour. Gently picked them up. The garment was obviously a chauffeur's jacket, cut in navy-blue serge, and it had some rubbed-out staining on the left shoulder and back. There were also a few spots on the left side of the cap, similarly rubbed out.

'Where did you find these?' Gently's voice betrayed his interest.

The super made an ironic gesture. 'Where does everything pop up? They were in a derelict shack in the carrs, about half a mile above Upper Wrackstead.'

'On which side of the river?'

'On the side opposite from you.'

Gently pulled out his map.

'I'd like the exact position.'

The super showed him impatiently. Hadn't he already investigated it?

'There aren't any prints, if that's what you're thinking about.'

'What's this line running up here?'

'It's a dyke from the river.'

'There'd be room to take a boat up?'

'There might, if it was small enough.'

'What about access to the road?'

'It's like you see – about quarter of a mile from this by-road between Wrackstead and Coleshill. It's a rough passage through the carrs, but you can get there all right.'

'And this shack – it isn't recent?'

'Not by fifty years it isn't. I'm told they grazed cattle there before the carrs grew up . . . that's when it was probably built.'

'Didn't look like he'd been camping there?'

'No.' The super frowned. 'There's only one sign that he'd been there, and that's the jacket and the cap.'

Gently nodded from a thoughtful distance. He folded his map and put it away.

'Well . . . that's my minor contribution! Now perhaps we can get to yours. You'll have talked to this Brent woman – what's she got to commit suicide about?'

'She thinks she knows who did it– '

'Oh does she, by the living thunder!'

'I said she *thinks* she knows . . . I'm not at all certain that she does. She wasn't around at the time and nobody seems to have got in touch with her.'

'Never mind! Who's her tip?'

Gently shrugged. 'She isn't giving us one. She was able to infer we hadn't made an arrest . . . I'm afraid she's going to be strictly uncooperative.'

The super said something naughty. 'She'll damn well change her mind about that! But just thinking she knows who did it . . . that's no reason to turn on the gas.'

'She thinks she's implicated . . . and she's in love with whoever it is.'

'You mean in love with the chauffeur?'

'Not necessarily. Paul Lammas fills the bill.'

The super stared shrewdly for a moment and then ruffled some report sheets which lay on his desk.

'I've been reading a copy of the statements you took this afternoon. I don't have to ask you what you've got from Paul Lammas. And I've been thinking, Gently. I've been thinking a lot!'

Gently inclined his head deferentially.

'To begin with, we agree that the chauffeur was only the trigger-puller on this job – I'm talking about Lammas' murder now. He may not even have pulled the trigger, but whether he did or not, there's somebody else behind him. Check?'

'Check.' Gently looked as though he might say something else, but he prevented himself. He'd better not rub it in!

'In the second place, we agree that whoever is behind the chauffeur may have succeeded in getting him out of the country – probably to some place from which he can't be extradited back again. Check?'

Gently hesitated. 'I'm not quite so struck with that theory as I was this morning.'

'How do you mean?' The super eyed him nastily.

'It's just a hunch . . . but I've a feeling he may be right under our noses.'

'You've got a lead?'

'No, nothing you can really call one.'

'Then damn it, man, stop trying to complicate the issue any further!' The super was really annoyed. 'I've spent all day coming round to your idea and now you want to slide out of it.'

'I'm sorry about that.'

'And it's the only one that fits the facts. If he hasn't skipped, where the blasted hell is he?'

Gently's shoulders hunched. 'I don't quite know.'

'And nor do I – and nor do five score policemen who've been raking the marshes for him. If it was Hicks who killed Annie Packer he'd be in a cell by now – but he isn't, and it wasn't! Do I have to go on my knees?'

Gently shrugged again and said nothing.

'Very well – we agree on that one. Hicks is where we'll never get him. That leaves us to deal with whoever was making use of him – and whoever did kill Annie Packer. Now by your own results we've narrowed it down to three, Marsh, Paul and Mrs Lammas, and what we've got to decide is whether we should charge one, two or all three of them. They were all on the spot. They all had good reasons! Perhaps you can tell me if you've got any favourites among those three.'

Gently shook his head. 'It works out pretty even. We can deduce that Linda Brent thinks it's Paul, but against that it was Mrs Lammas who was inquiring where her husband would be and her prints were on the gun-drawer. On the other hand this Marsh would seem to have the strongest motive and looking forward to Annie Packer, he's the only one with sufficient physical strength to have handled the body as it must have been handled. No ... I haven't any favourites. On the evidence, I wouldn't dare have.'

'Then we know where we are.' The super's jaw jutted decisively. 'We shall charge all three with conspiracy to murder and to my way of thinking that's just about the truth.'

'But it won't stand up.'

'Why won't it stand up?'

'Because you haven't got Hicks . . . a good defence will simply romp home. They can hang it on him in just the way it's been planned. If you can't get Hicks you'll never get a verdict.'

'They may rat on each other – it's been known before today.'

'But you can't bank on that.'

'And there's bound to be some other evidence!'

'I'd like to see it before making a charge.'

The super didn't snarl, although he looked as though he would have liked to. But he knew sense when he heard it and this, he knew, was sense. So he contented himself with putting a band-saw edge into the tone of his next remark.

'Then if we never get Hicks, what in the thirty-seven blue moons of Gehenna are we something-well going to do?'

Gently produced a peppermint cream from somewhere and began chewing it with insubordinate slowness.

'I haven't got a solution . . . I only know I'm not happy with the facts. Of course there's some routine-work we haven't covered yet, like the outgoings from Mrs Lammas' banking accounts, and what Marsh's servants know about his movements last night. I'm not expecting too much from either source. For the rest I just don't know. I've got a hunch that there's a penny due to drop.'

'But what are you going to *do*, man?' exploded the super, not at the moment a great backer of hunches.

'I'm going to charge Linda Brent . . . can I borrow your phone?'

The super watched him malevolently as he dialled a number. There had been times before when Gently had made the great man want to tear his close-cropped hair . . .

'This is Chief Inspector Gently, Central Office, CID. I've a statement for you . . . give me a machine, will you? This evening Linda Brent, etc., wanted by the Police for questioning in connection with the murder of James William Lammas, was taken into custody and charged with conspiring to defraud while an employee of Lammas Wholesalers Ltd.'

'You'll never make it stick, Gently!' rapped the super as the phone was replaced.

Gently supplied himself with another peppermint cream.

'I don't really mind if I don't,' he replied wearily.

CHAPTER FOURTEEN

M OVE IN LAMMAS case – Gently Charges Linda Brent. It was bannered beautifully across the morning paper which lay by Gently's cup of tea.

Outside, the river-dwellers were stirring about their business. Pedro was off fruit-picking again, Thatcher was digging for worms, the slattern was getting off to school her own and Cheerful Annie's offspring.

'I see you're findin' out things, sir,' sniffed Mrs Grey as she set down the breakfast bacon. She had always a tear to command since the rumour about her nephew being seen had got about.

'We do our best, Mrs Grey.'

Gently beat Dutt to the crispest-looking rasher.

'You haven't found my poor sister's boy, sir, not with all your tryin' – and I don't reckon you will, now, either.'

'Oh, I don't know, Mrs Grey. It's surprising how they turn up.'

'I know, sir. But don't it stand to reason? He's done away with himself, that's what he's done, and I say Heaven forgive them what druv him to it!'

And the poor lady went out in a storm of tears.

Gently made a face as he took the mustard.

'Another theorist, Dutt . . . and not a bad one at that.'

'Yessir . . . we'd look silly if he comes to the surface somewhere.'

'We'd look sillier still if he had a .22 bullet in him!'

The sun was beaming down with its customary splendour. Nothing was going to spoil this paragon of Junes. On the wicked and the innocent alike it spread its glamour. Colour seemed a new invention, the air a crystalline liquid. Even Thatcher had a romantic look, scruffing away with a handleless trowel – he might have been some old earth god about his masonic delvings.

'What's three half-crowns worth to you?'

Thatcher looked up quickly.

'We want the use of a dinghy . . . yours will do, if it doesn't leak too much.'

'Ah, but wait yew a minute, bor!'

Nobody made snap deals with Thatcher.

'Dew yew want it all day that might come a bit more . . . tha's what yew might call the Season at this end of June!'

But Gently didn't want it all day, and the seven and six changed hands. Dutt was allotted the oars, Gently seated himself in the stern and Thatcher shoved them off with professional panache.

The river was shut-in all the way to the dyke and the shack where the jacket had been found. Snaked roots of alder reached out from either bank, screens of reed, bramble and wild currant formed a barrier to the eye.

The carrs were a secret place. They warned you off with their stockaded boundaries. To get in there you must be prepared to have the clothes torn off your back, the shoes from your feet, and you must suffer beating, scratching, soaking and an overlay of mud . . .

'Not a place one would choose for a man-hunt, Dutt.'

'No, sir . . . you takes the words out of me mouth.'

'But a good place to hide something, other things being equal.'

Gently had the map on his knee and it was necessary equipment. They went past the dyke twice before spotting where it lay. Its mouth was concealed by a floating reed-hover, but even had it not been one would have had difficulty in recognizing the grown-over inlet.

'Get your head down, sir!'

Gently didn't need telling. The alder twigs whipped and stung them as Dutt poled in with one oar. In the slip of a dinghy they had to crouch double and every few yards the inch of keel was touching sugarily on the mud. But they weren't sticking fast – that was the point to be proved! Yard by yard, they were continuing to find clean water ahead. You could get a dinghy up there. Especially if there was only one of you . . .

The dyke came to an end as indefinitely as it had begun, simply oozing out of existence in mud and rush jungle. Gently scrutinized what could theoretically be called the bank.

'Of course they didn't look for this . . . and of course they didn't find it!'

He reached over into a mass of mint and meadow-sweet and tugged something out. It was a long, straight rod of willow, which had been pushed slantwise into the greasy peat.

'One should always moor a dinghy.'

He shoved the rod back again.

'Now let's see if we can find anything else they didn't notice!'

If it had been trying in the dinghy, it was doubly trying out of it. After half a dozen steps, one just forgot about dry feet. And there were brambles like saws, and nettles like wasps' nests, and the moist, enclosed air made perspiration start at the slightest exertion. There was a track of sorts, or at all events a line of least resistance. Along it had recently sploshed a number of police-issue boots but they weren't responsible for everything. Gently noticed signs of earlier passages. Here there was a snapped twig with leaves which had withered, there a turned-back bramble trying to grow in its original direction.

Not recent at all . . . those dry leaves weren't properly developed.

'Blimey – just give me the Commercial Road!'

Dutt was mopping a streaming face and snatching at the rubbish in his hair.

'No wonder the charlies round here live in rubber boots – it's a marvel they ain't born wiv webbed feet!'

Gently grinned commiseration. 'Stick it out, Dutt . . . it's all experience.'

'Hi know, sir – and I hopes it's worth it!'

'Here's the shack now . . . but I wish we'd been here yesterday.'

The shack was as the super had described it. It

consisted of three sides framed in rough timber and filled with reeds, while some aged reed-thatch served for a roof. It was built on ground that was a little higher and therefore a little drier than the carrs surrounding it. This feature seemed to have made it rather popular with five score of policeman.

Gently sighed as he cautiously approached it. Yet what was he hoping to find there, after all? Perhaps he was only being fascinated by yet one more fact that didn't quite fit . . . wanting to worry at it, to double-check it, to wrest sense out of it somehow. Because there was no doubt that it didn't fit. It would only have fitted if Hicks had been hiding there. *Then* one could show how he had slipped out in a dinghy . . . how he had been secretly provisioned by his aunt . . . how he had come to kill Cheerful Arnie. It would have been full of possibilities! Only Hicks hadn't been hiding there. You had only to look at the shack.

Three parts of the floor was raising a lovely bed of nettles and the fourth part wasn't large enough to have slept a good-sized dog.

Gently stood still, staring at it. He was getting depressed and irritated by this perpetual check-mating. At every turn a contradiction was slapped across his face, a twit given to his intolerable ignorance. Was he going to fall down on this case? Had he run into a plan which was going to circumvent him, in all his wisdom?

A plan . . . that was the one thing his opponents couldn't hide. Lammas' murder hadn't been a brilliant piece of improvisation, it wasn't done on the spur of the moment. It looked like that, but it wasn't. Perhaps that was its weak spot, the flank which he could turn. You looked back to Easter, for instance. So many trails had started there. It was about Easter when Lammas hired the yacht. It was about Easter when he booked the bungalow. It was at Easter when Paul had threatened his mother with exposure. It was about Easter when Lammas began his unexplained mid-week trips. What was the interaction there . . . who had betrayed which to whom? Paul? Pauline? And the hiring of the yacht itself, what had Lammas been up to with that? Who had he really been expecting to meet when he took the *Harrier* up Ollby Dyke?

Out of a haze of abstraction Gently suddenly realized that he was looking at something, something very small and apparently out of place. It was a little shred of gold paper. It was caught between a horizontal timber and the reeds behind it. Quickly he bent to examine it more closely.

Torn edges . . . a wisp of label adhering . . . the back soiled with a greasy brown substance.

He gazed at it bemusedly for a moment, its significance dawning slowly. Then, in a sudden flash, the full comprehension began to arrive.

'*Dutt!*'

He couldn't quite keep the excitement out of his voice.

'Dutt – look at this! Come and tell me what you make of it!'

The sergeant came squelching across, a lugubrious expression on his face. There was a thrill in Gently's voice not to be denied, but the little strip of paper seemed scanty reason for such enthusiasm.

'Looks like a bit of toffee-paper, sir.'

'Toffee-paper, my foot!'

'I seen plenty just like it, sir—'

'Not like this piece, Dutt!'

Almost as though it were a holy relic he was guiding it into an envelope, hardly allowing himself to touch it, even with the blade of his pocket-knife.

'Dutt, we've as good as got him!'

His voice was trembling with suppressed exultation.

'It fits like a glove . . . I must have been mad not to see it before!'

'But what's it all about, sir?'

'. . . *about?* You have to ask me?'

'Well I might be hexceptional dense, sir, but that's just toffee-paper to *me!*'

Gently chuckled as he straighted up. His eye had that far-distant look which came at moments when mystery was ceasing to be mystery, when the picture he sought had begun to take shape.

'Come on . . . this isn't enough, Dutt! There should be something more solid. And now we know what we're looking for, we may know where to find it – even if we aren't quite certain about the bloke who put it there!'

'Then we don't know who it was, sir?'

'We do, Dutt – and we don't.'

'Couldn't you put it a little plainer, sir?'

'It'll be plain enough before long!'

He set off back to the dinghy without vouchsafing another word. Dutt shook his head in sorrow and followed his senior with oozing steps. He wasn't usually a stupid policeman – what had he missed on this amphibious excursion?

Upper Wrackstead Dyke was a peaceful spot as the dinghy came sculling back to its moorings. The children were at school, the river-dwellers about their business and the sun shining hot on cottage, willows and boats. Only Thatcher was brought to his cabin door by the sound of the approaching oars.

'Blast, bor!' he commented. '*Yew* din't want a boot for long!'

Gently shrugged and cast a speculative eye over the deserted scene. So quiet it was, so still.

'An look what yew've done t'her – she in't half in a pickle! Yew din't tell me yew'd be a-jammin' about in the carrs!'

'Here's half a crown for the mess.'

'Ah, an' worth evra penna.'

'What's that wire-net contraption with handle you've got on the cabin roof?'

Thatcher turned about to look. His cabin roof was a depository for all sorts of superannuated junk.

'Yew mean this here?'

'Yes – what's it for?'

'W'blast, tha's a dydle, and they use it for dydlin' out dykes.'

'You can dredge in the mud with it?'

'W'yes, tha's what tha's for.'

'I'd like to borrow it . . . it's worth another five bob.'

With the dydle securely lashed to the roof-rack, they set out in the Wolseley. Gently was in an effervescent, schoolboy mood. You would almost have thought he was off on a treat.

'We're going to Ollby, sir?'

Dutt was a little put out by his senior's unwillingness to confide in him.

'Yes, Dutt – Ollby ho!'

'You reckon we'll find something, sir?'

'I reckon we stand a chance, Dutt . . . a very good chance!'

Dutt jiffled a little. How like Gently it was, this irritating mysteriousness when he thought he had the scent!

'Might I ask what we'll be looking for, sir?'

Gently grinned into his driving-mirror.

'Let me put it to you, Dutt . . . I like to benefit by your Cockney common sense! Suppose you'd just popped off Lammas and you were going ahead with the cremation programme. Would you, or wouldn't you be in a bit of a hurry?'

'I'd be in a hurry, sir . . . too flipping true I would!'

'And being in this hurry, suppose you discovered something on Lammas which, if even a trace of it were found, would give the game away – and which might not burn satisfactorily. What would you do with it?'

Dutt hesitated cautiously.

'Somethink which might be missed, sir?'

'No – quite the contrary – somethink which would never be missed.'

'Then I'd sling it overboard, sir, always provided it would sink nicely.'

Gently nodded complacently.

'That's just how I argued.'

'But what is this somethink, sir?'

'Ah . . . that remains to be seen!'

Nothing had changed at Ollby Quay, except that the wreck was missing and the smell of burning grown stale. Now that the wreck was gone the charred trees seemed a little unreal and ashamed of themselves. They presented such a woeful contrast to the smiling reed-and-alder bounded pool with its rampant lilies, its white-flowered plants and its domestic water-hens.

'What a place to commit murder!'

Gently brooded over it pensively a moment as he unbuttoned his jacket.

'You'd think people would have more sense . . . it's only a failure who would kill! Here, give me the net. I've always fancied my chances with one.'

Dutt willingly surrendered the dydle, which, with its generous twelve feet of handle, was no sinecure.

'We may have to get a boat up here – it depends on what sort of sling the fellow had.'

Gently considered the spot where the yacht had lain, then dipped in at the far side of the dyke on which the quay fronted. The water didn't run deep, but there was some exquisitely resistance-less mud beneath it. Some business it was going to be, finding anything in that lot . . .

He trawled off a netful and drew it laboriously to the bank.

'Roll your sleeves up, Dutt – you're in this too!'

Together they went through it, getting muddied to the elbows. It had a peculiarly viscous quality, that mud; you knew you'd been amongst it. And the sum total of the catch was a number of fresh-water mussel shells . . .

Gently tried again. One really couldn't expect impossible luck! He trawled along the dyke carefully and systematically, trying to cover the whole area of the dyke adjacent to where the yacht had been. And slowly the grey-drying pile on the bank grew larger, and Dutt and himself muddier, and the collection of mussel shells more representative. There wasn't even an old tin to diversify the proceedings. Not even some broken glass.

'Have a go with the net, sir?'

It was anything for a change.

Gently wiped a streaming brow with a muddy hand and passed over the dydle.

'I've just about covered the dyke . . . try your luck in the pool. Come to think of it, it's probably the likelier place.'

He scrubbed his hands in the grass and got out his pipe. There was no doubt that a professional dydler would earn all he could make at the job! He ought to have requisitioned a boat and some Constables . . . that would have been the way to tackle it. But when you got hold of a lucky break it gave you a feeling of inevitability.

Dutt brought in his first netful. Even the mussel shells were getting scarce. Solemnly they felt their way through the atrocious mixture, the obscene and gluti- nous mixture. And then . . . and then . . .

'Here sir, would this be anythink?'

It was Dutt who made the strike. From a handful of mud he was separating a smallish, horse-shoe-shaped object, part of which gleamed rosily through its porridge-like envelopment.

Gently almost held his breath.

'Go on, Dutt . . . scrape the mud off it!'

Dutt obliged, with a look of perplexity.

'Now – you tell me! What have we got?'

'Well . . . it's half a set of choppers!'

'Yes, Dutt . . . half a set of choppers – and they're going to hang a certain party!'

He seized on the object in triumph and straightened a back which had suddenly ceased to ache. Here it was, the unarguable proof – the final fact, the fact that hung!

Dutt stared dumbly at the muddied denture. 'But I don't quite see, sir—' he was beginning, when two things happened which he didn't see either. The first was a vicious hiss from across the pool and a rattling crash in the twigs behind them. The second was Gently's tackle that sent him flying face-first into the mud.

'Keep flat!' bawled Gently, 'Keep your head down on the ground. If you show a couple of inches you'll maybe stop a .22 bullet between the eyes!'

The rotten planks of the quay gave a modicum of cover, but they looked uncomfortably penetrable. Gently eased himself towards them until he could peer through one of the gaps. Not a sound, not a movement came from the direction from which the shot had been fired. Over there it was all green reeds and a single, scrubby alder. To get there one would have to skirt the dyke and make a rush through the slopping marsh and tangled under-

213

growth . . . a perfect target all the way. He had picked his spot well, the man with the gun.

'Can you see him, sir?'

Dutt was spitting the mud out of his mouth.

'No, Dutt — and we shan't! He doesn't want to be seen.'

'You don't think he's hooked it, sir, after taking a pot?'

'Not him . . . this is too important. He's got us on his list.'

By way of testing the hypothesis Gently reached across for his jacket, which was lying folded under a bush. He rolled it into a tight wad and suddenly poked it up above the level of the planks. Almost simultaneously a bullet kicked it out of his hand. . .

'That's tidy shooting with a silenced .22!'

'Here, but wait a minute, sir!'

Dutt had crawled up beside him.

'We've got a banger too — I never signed in that Webley yesterday!'

Gently stared. 'You mean we've got it here?'

'Yessir. Right up there in me pocket.'

'In your pocket!' Gently craned his head. Dutt's jacket was hanging on a snag, about three yards behind them.

'If we can get that down we'll have this geezer in a jam, sir. It's the old .38, and I know which I'd sooner be behind!'

'Also it'll make a noise.' A gleam came into Gently's eye. 'But how the devil are we going to get it down, with Davy Crockett sitting in the rushes?'

Tantalizingly the jacket hung there, only just hooked on to a snag. A quick spring . . . a sweep of the arm! But a vigilant bullet was waiting for just such a move.

'We'll have to knock it off with the dydle, Dutt.'

Dutt pulled a face. 'A fine mess it'll make.'

'So would a bullet in the back – even a little .22!'

Gently squirmed towards the dydle, trying to keep himself perfectly flat. He couldn't quite have succeeded, since when he was halfway towards it there was a warning hiss and something plucked a loose part of his shirt.

'That lad's quite a marksman. I wonder what he'll be like when someone's firing back!'

But he managed to get the dydle and tow it back to where Dutt was crouching.

Now came the difficult part – raising the dydle to the level of the jacket. Dydles were no light-weights and the amount of leverage one could get while in a prone position was inconsiderable, to say the least.

'Let's anchor the butt-end under the planks.'

It was done and they both braced themselves.

'We want to get it first time – we shall have to show ourselves a bit!'

How they managed it remained a mystery. A couple of bullets sliced by as the dydle wavered in mid-air. Then it fell with a thump, a white flake carved from the haft . . . and wonder of wonders, Dutt's jacket had come down on top of it! Gently hooked it up with his toe. Yes . . . the Webley was still in the pocket. He slipped off the safety-catch and spun the magazine.

'To the left of that tree, sir – I see the rushes twitching!'

Gently had seen them too, but it wasn't at the rushes that he aimed. When the healthy crash of the .38 rang out a bough shivered in the solitary alder . . . and there followed the splashes of hastily retreating footsteps.

'Let me get after him, sir!' Dutt was on his feet in a moment. 'Just give me that gun – I'll teach him the way to shoot at people!'

Gently signified a negative and rose more leisuredly.

'You'd be *easy* meat, Dutt. He couldn't ask anything better than for you to follow him in there.'

'But we can't let him go, sir – he's the bloke what we're after! And if he's in that marsh we can stow him up with a cordon—!'

Gently shook his head again and clicked the safety back on the Webley.

'No cordons, Dutt, and no following . . . there's been enough bloodshed round here already. And I want him alive when I get him. I doubt whether I should, if we stowed him up with a cordon.'

'But you can't just let him go!' It outraged all Dutt's police-instincts. 'If we don't get him now we may never have another chance, sir. And don't forget we never see him – we can't swear to who he was if we don't catch him!'

Gently smiled a frosty smile. He weighed the Webley in his hand.

'But we know who he was, Dutt . . . we knew from the very first bullet. And we know where to find him – *because he doesn't know we know!* Now let's forget about the drama and do some routine work on this denture. When it comes to the fun and games, you'll get your share along with the rest!'

216

CHAPTER FIFTEEN

THERE WAS A little more animation about Upper Wrackstead in the middle of the afternoon. For one thing it was early closing in the village and some of the river-dwellers worked there. For another, it was the hour of gossip, when all the chores ought to have been done. And then there were freelances like Pedro, who couldn't make up their minds to work in the afternoon and others like Thatcher, who didn't work anyway.

Quite a number were there to witness Gently drive up alone in the police Wolseley.

He locked the doors casually and took his time about getting off the dydle. A couple of kids stopped chasing each other to stand and drink in the spectacle.

'When are y'going t'lock up Mrs Grey, mister?'

Gently grinned at them amiably.

'She did for old Annie – she did, din't she?'

'Sid – Teddy!'

It was the slattern screeching from her companion hatch.

'Just yew come away from there an stop cheekin' the pleeceman!'

Reluctantly the youngsters heeded the voice of fate.

Gently shouldered the dydle and humped it over to Thatcher's houseboat. The gentleman in question lay snoring on his cabin-top, his hands clasped sedately over his shapely paunch. Not far away sat Pedro. He was playing sadly on his concertina. The nostalgic Italian music seemed somehow to harmonize with Thatcher's magnificent snore.

'Oi!'

Thatcher broke off in mid-thunder.

'I've brought your dydle back.'

The recumbent figure sat up slowly and scratched its ear.

'Yew din't have to wake me up . . . I was havin' a lovela sleep! An what ha'y' been dewin' with my dydle – tha's got a lump took outta the handle!'

Gently shrugged and handed it up to him.

'It's fair wear-and-tear.'

'Not a lump like that i'nt! I suppose yew'll tell me a pike bit it?'

'You wouldn't be so far out.'

Gently moved a few steps towards Cheerful Annie's wherry and Pedro, his legs dangling over the bows, stopped playing a moment. But Gently seemed to change his mind. He turned back to where Thatcher was tenderly replacing the dydle with his other junk.

'Ah well . . . just one more bit of business! I want the dinghy again.'

'What arter the way yew messed her up this mornin?'

'I shan't mess her up this afternoon.'

Thatcher hesitated doubtfully. The nick out of the dydle seemed to have dropped his opinion of policemen by a few points.

'That i'nt them carrs again, I s'pose?'

'No – it's that old mill across on the other bank.'

'Yew can mess a boot up there, dew yew're got a mind to.'

'You come with me and keep me out of mischief.'

Thatcher fingered the obnoxious bullet-score pointedly. It was almost humorous to watch his mind working . . .

'Verra well, my man! Five bob – take it or leave it.'

'It's too much, you old sinner. But I'll take it – if you row!'

Thatcher climbed down from the cabin-top and drew in the dinghy. Everyone was watching as Gently stepped aboard. Thatcher winked at them ponderously over the policeman's shoulder . . . *he'd* got his head screwed on, the wink seemed to say.

'Are yew all set, ole partna?'

Gently was arranging his feet.

'Then here w'go, an' the best of luck!'

On the bows of the wherry Pedro continued to play his sentimental tune. It followed them for quite a distance as the dinghy turned downstream.

'I've just about finished, ole partna.'

Gently could slip easily into an imitation of Thatcher's vernacular.

'We'll ha done by s'arternoon, an leave yew all t'get on with it, together.'

Thatcher wasn't going to be hurried. He rowed with a slow, steady, waterman's stroke which made even a dinghy seem monumental. And Gently wasn't in a hurry. He trailed stubby fingers in the sun-warm water. Two middle-aged men, one comfortably disreputable, the other comfortably respectable, you expected them to pull into the bank at any moment and to get out their rods. Why else would they be sauntering downstream in that antedeluvian dinghy?

'I reckon yew b'long here somehow, bor . . . yew don't pick our natter up that easa.'

'W'blast, there's nothin tew it. I onla got to listen t'soma yew carryin' on.'

Thatcher gave a little chuckle and twisted his head appreciatively. Not many foreigners could master the sly, dry North-shire tongue with its pace and familiar lilt and abundance of glottal stops.

'Well then, who was't, arter all?' he inquired, lifting an oar to accommodate a patch of floating weed.

Gently hunched his shoulders lazily.

'We'll know in a bit . . . my sergeant is going to pick him up.'

'I'll have a quid on that was Joe Hicks.'

'I'd take you, too, if I was a betting man.'

Thatcher chuckled again and rowed on methodically. He wasn't doing so badly out of Gently, when you came to weigh it up. Fifteen bob in the morning, five in the afternoon.

'But what about all that monna?'

The thought of cash had recalled the box of notes.

'Aren't the kids goin to ha' that now, when yew've got the bloke yew want?'

Gently fed himself a peppermint cream. 'It's still stolen property.'

'But blast – yew can stretch a point! Yew know their ole man's dewin' time.'

'They'll be taken care of . . . don't worry about that.'

'But that monna was theirs. That say so on the box!'

'The person who was being so lavish would have to prove his title.'

Thatcher rested on his oars. The point really seemed to worry him. His grizzled brows contracted as he wrestled with the problem.

'But are yew *pos'tive* that was stolen?' he asked at last, 'ha yew foun' out where that come from?'

'W'no, ole partna – but it's a hundred to one it was stolen from Mr Lammas.'

'Well, there y'are, then!' A hundred to one was nothing to Thatcher. 'Dew yew aren't pos'tive, why not give them little kiddoes the benefit o' th' doubt?'

'To be honest, I wish I could . . . but it isn't in my power.'

Thatcher studied him seriously before dipping his oars again. There was a penetration in his hazel eyes surprising in its calm power. 'Yew got yourself mixed up with a rum lot, bor, I'm buggered if yew ha'nt!' he observed sadly.

Gently gave an almost imperceptible shrug. 'We're all a rum lot, bor . . . there i'nt much t'chewse atween us,' he replied.

They had rounded the bend which cut off Upper Wrackstead and entered the long, reed-lined Mill Reach. At the other end was a bend which would bring

Wrackstead Bridge and village into view, but the Reach itself gave no premonition of these nearby haunts of men. From a boat, its solitude was complete. One saw nothing but the tall reeds and scrub marsh trees above them. The majestic, rusty brick tower of a ruined drainage-mill pointed, if possible, the sense of remoteness and desolation. Even under a June sun, even in the presence of some passing holiday craft.

'Yew aren't a-goin' to tell me yew don't know who done that job, jus' when yew're going to lay hands on him.'

Thatcher was still puzzling about it. The police worked in mysterious ways!

'I know who did it.' Gently was talking softly, as though to himself. 'Only nobody would believe me . . . unless I produced the man.'

'Then how dew your bloke know who he's arrestin', dew yew han't told him?'

'I've told him where he'll find him. There won't be any room for mistake.'

Thatcher brooded on it for a moment.

'Don't that put yew in a rum position?'

'It could do, I suppose . . . if I were inclined to let it.'

Their eyes came together, Gently's mild ones, Thatcher's questioning.

'Dew he knew what yew've told me, yew might not have so long to go, ole partna.'

'Yes . . . he's handy with a gun.'

'Ah, an' don't care if he use it.'

'They get handier all the time . . . that's the reason one has to stop them.'

Thatcher slewed round in his seat to bawl out a speeding motor-cruiser. The offending helmsman was completely silenced by such a barrage of pungent English.

'But what sort of blokes d'yew reckon they are, who go about killin' other people?'

Now they were getting near the mill and one could see the low, square doorway.

'They're all a bit twisted . . . they've had a left-handed deal.' There was a dyke and a sluice-gate, and a sunken houseboat in the dyke.

'Yew mean they're ordinara people?'

'Yes . . . ordinara people.'

'Onla suffns pushed'm into't.'

'Suffns pushed, and they've pushed back.'

Thatcher turned the dinghy with his oar and it floated gently into the mill-dyke. Above the sluice-gate, grotesque, sun-bleached, rose the ruined paddle-wheel, like a symbol from a lost world.

'So yew aren't realla agin'm . . .?'

'No . . . I just want to stop them.'

'Yew're goin t'give'm another push.'

'It isn't me who does the pushing.'

The dinghy touched on the bank. Thatcher shipped his oars with a quick, suddenly irritable movement. Gently continued to sit trailing his fingers. About the mill there was an air of unnatural quietness.

'W'here she is, dew yew want to see her.'

Thatcher's voice had taken on a roughness. Gently nodded, but didn't stir.

'Would there be any works left in her?'

Thatcher silently tied the painter.

Reluctantly, Gently climbed out on to the bank. In front of the mill it was firm and clear. Behind and beside it a thick growth of bush willow hid the surrounding marshes, but just here it was rough, hummocky turf.

'Tha's the door dew yew're goin in.'

Thatcher had climbed out too and was standing close behind him.

'Mind y'head as yew go through . . . they dint build it t'take six-footers.'

Gently went forward towards the gap and Thatcher followed a pace in the rear.

But before they could enter there was an interruption. The smart, uniformed figure of Superintendent Walker emerged from the mill. And along with him, ducking their heads, came five other people – Mrs Lammas, Paul, Pauline, Hansom and Dutt.

An assembly of eight, they stood staring at each other on the hummocky turf in front of the mill.

'Gently, I'd like to know what the devil you're playing at!'

The super began angrily and then broke off, aware of an undefinable tension which had somehow sprung up.

What was it? What had happened?

Everyone was standing there like statues!

'Gently, I might as well tell you . . .'

Gently wasn't listening to him. Nobody was listening to him. Pauline Lammas had covered her face, Paul was staring frantically in front of him, his mother's eyes were ferocious burning coals. But why? What was causing it? Nobody had as much as spoken a syllable!

'Gently . . .'

The super glared from one to another, desperately trying to comprehend the unbearable strain. It couldn't last, this! Something would have to give somewhere. They stood as though rooted by a frightful supernatural power – Gently too, poised on his toes, and Thatcher, looking as though he had seen the devil.

And still it went on!

Sweat began beading on the super's brow.

He wanted to say something, to take charge somehow. But his throat had gone dry and his brain seemed paralysed. He looked at Hansom. Hansom's mouth was open to its fullest extent. He looked at Dutt. The sergeant had a sort of grinning frown on his face. Had they all gone mad? Was it the super who was mad?

'Someone . . . somebody!'

He couldn't recognize that croak as his own.

'I'm asking you . . .!'

It might have been a scene from another planet.

And then, very, very slowly, something did begin to happen. At first it was little gasping coughs, almost as though somebody were muttering to himself, but then it increased both in volume and pitch.

Paul was laughing. But what laughter!

With his lips drawn tight across his teeth, he was sending out great rippling screams of laughter, laughter that iced the blood in the super's veins.

'Stop it – stop that row!'

Paul only shrieked the louder.

'Slap his face . . . we've got to stop him!'

It didn't occur to the super to slap Paul's face himself.

He daren't move either . . . now! He was petrified like the others. Instinctively he knew that a movement would trigger off something.

'*Ha, ha, ha, ha!*'

From bank to bank the crazy laughter echoed.

In the hot afternoon sun the super shivered and sweated at the same time. Was nothing going to break it? Would it go on for ever?

If only one understood . . . if one knew who . . .!

When the end came, it was almost an anti-climax. The enormous tension snapped as inexplicably as it had begun. There was a cry from Dutt, a sudden flurry of movement. A heavy body went one way and a silenced .22 Beretta the other.

At the same moment, as though part of the same mechanism, Mrs Lammas struck her son a blow on the face, a blow that well nigh felled him to the ground.

'Get the cuffs on him, Dutt!'

'Yessir. You bet, sir!'

Gently had not been tender and Thatcher was in no condition to resist. Over by herself Pauline Lammas was sobbing brokenly, Paul was gasping and holding his face. Mrs Lammas stood exactly as she had stood during the whole incident. Her eyes were fixed on Thatcher as though she would turn him into stone.

'But who in the hell is this fellow?'

The super spoke dazedly, still trying to catch up.

Gently motioned to Dutt.

'Get him up on his feet.'

'I'm asking you, Gently!'

'In a minute – get him up!'

It was anti-climax now and still incomprehensible. The super couldn't place Thatcher. He just didn't belong in those handcuffs!

'You understand what I'm saying?'

Thatcher was breathless, but he understood.

'Very well, I take it you do – and you must know what to expect! I hereby charge you, James William Lammas, with the murder of your chauffeur, Joseph Hicks, and I must warn you that anything you say may be taken down in writing and used in evidence.'

A bemused silence followed this statement. It was so completely bizarre, so unreal. Yet Thatcher wasn't trying to contradict the charge and the silenced Beretta lay bearing mute witness on the trampled turf.

'You're crazy . . . it *couldn't* be him!'

Hansom found his tongue.

'Lammas was a slim type – this bloke could give him five stone. And he was ten years younger! I tell you there isn't any resemblance.'

'That's right, Gently!' Hansom had taken the words out of the super's mouth. 'I've seen Lammas' photograph and he wasn't remotely like this chap.'

Grimly Gently approached the heavy-breathing Thatcher. A clumsy finger hooked into the seamy waistcoat and ripped off the buttons from top to bottom. Then it was the turn of the twill shirt, and then the cotton vest.

'There . . . that's how he got the figure!'

Through the tattered garments protruded a stuffed linen bag, expertly moulded into shape and attached with tapes.

'And this is where he got the ten years!'

Gently pulled out his handkerchief and dabbed the corner of Thatcher's eye. A browny-red stain of greasepaint appeared on the white fabric . . .

'And if you still aren't satisfied—'

He spun savagely on his heel.

'—ask his daughter there, who was prepared to be an accessory for him! Ask his son, who despised his lack of spirit! Or ask his wife, who in effect destroyed him! They'll tell you who he is – or one of them will!'

He paused, his eye fixed on Mrs Lammas. The hate that flared at him was like a glimpse of hell-fire. But she didn't say anything. Neither did Paul say anything. It was Pauline who ran sobbing to throw herself into her father's arms.

'Daddy – oh daddy! I did my best!'

Somehow, in spite of the handcuffs, he managed to stroke her short, fair hair.

'I guessed what had happened . . . I wouldn't tell them!'

'Don't cry, little girl.'

'Daddy . . . I did my best!'

'You've always done your best . . .'

It was Lammas speaking now. They had heard the last of Thatcher. His voice was inexpressibly soft and kindly, but his eyes were staring vacantly and he didn't look down at his daughter.

'Oh daddy – oh daddy!'

'Little girl . . . you mustn't cry.'

Gently bit his lip painfully and touched her on the shoulder. She broke away directly, as if acknowledging her powerlessness to resist. He hesitated by the pinioned man.

'But why did you have to do it?'

Lammas shook his head bewilderedly.

'Christ knows . . . Christ only knows.'

'You're a decent sort of chap . . .'

'I got the idea . . . it fascinated me. Christ knows! I *had* to do it.'

'All right then – we know where we are!'

The super's bark was unnecessarily biting.

'You admit you're Lammas – you've heard the chief inspector charge you. If you've anything to say, just remember that it's evidence. I'm not paying any attention to that last remark of yours.'

Lammas nodded without looking at him.

'I intend to make a statement.'

'You can do that back at headquarters, though if you'll take my advice—'

He pulled himself up. Policemen didn't give that sort of advice!

'We've got the cars back on the road. Hansom, get this man away!'

What the super wanted to do was to regularize the situation, but the official note, once lost, seemed strangely unwilling to resume itself. He stood almost to attention as he watched them file away. First there was Lammas, conducted by Dutt and Hansom. Then followed Pauline, her head bent in sobs. Finally came Mrs Lammas and Paul, the latter still looking like a madman. Mrs Lammas walked in frozen state. She was there by constraint . . . this scene was unutterably beneath her!

As they disappeared behind the mill the super slowly relaxed from his pose.

'I've seen some jobs in my time . . . I've seen one or two!'

He turned on Gently with a sudden fierceness.

'You've made his coffin and screwed him down in it. You swine, Gently . . . you bloody swine!'

Gently nodded to the flowing stream. It wasn't ever much fun, being a policeman.

CHAPTER SIXTEEN

'NOW WE KNOW why he killed Annie Packer.'
Lammas had made a long, long statement. In the super's office it was stuffy and warm in spite of two open windows and the obstinate issue from Gently's sand-blast didn't improve matters a bit. Down below the evening traffic was still busy in the street. A moment ago they'd been turning out of the theatre. In the pub across the way, no doubt, the cloth had gone up ten minutes ago.

'What else could he do?'

Gently looked tired and bored, standing by the window. There was a nasty taste in his mouth. He had never been involved in a case he liked less, or been so sickened by his triumph. Yet Lammas had tried to kill him, too. And at the mill there'd been another bullet with his number on it.

'When she caught him with his clothes off there was only one answer. And that's why I couldn't find any blood – he shot her in the cabin.'

'We'll find some blood – now we know where to look for it. And the bullet too, I daresay.'

The super hadn't much kick in him either. He was sitting hunched up, his hands dug into his pockets. It wasn't the way a super ought to sit, but for once in a while he was looking as though he couldn't care less.

'D'you think he told the truth about pulling the gun this afternoon?'

'Yes . . . he couldn't have gunned the lot of us. I was afraid of what he might do.'

'It'd have saved a lot of money.'

'I couldn't take the risk.'

'Would you have let him if you could?'

Gently made a meaningless gesture.

'We don't play God at our level . . . it's higher up you meet the divinities.'

He pulled on his pipe. It was obvious that he didn't want to talk. He'd done his job . . . he'd got to write his report. Apart from that, he'd have liked to have forgotten the whole thing.

But of course . . . he would have to tell his tale!

That's why the four of them were hanging on there, instead of going off to supper and bed. And in a way, he did want to talk. Just as Lammas had wanted to confess. When you talked you involved other people . . . you crept back out of the unbearable loneliness of experience.

'How about some coffee?'

The super pressed a button.

'Let's have some sandwiches too — come to think of it, I haven't eaten since lunch-time.'

Down there, they wouldn't know anything about Lammas' arrest until they got the morning papers.

★   ★   ★

232

The sandwiches were tongue and the coffee the brand of coffee that only superintendents get out of police canteens. Gently felt better after the snack. There was a sort of humanity in food and drink . . .

'Now – getting back to the beginning of this affair.'

He was sitting in his favourite way with the chair back to front. Dutt was stuck away in a corner, Hansom near the desk, his long legs sprawling. They hadn't put the light on – it wasn't really necessary.

'What stuck out like a sore thumb was that week on the yacht. It couldn't be explained – there was no adequate reason for it. Lammas had carefully planned things so that he had a week of grace before inquiries began, yet here he was, openly hanging about, almost making certain that someone took notice of him. You can argue that not many people on the Broads knew him and that he kept well clear of Wrackstead – but against that you've got to remember that he hired a Wrackstead boat and gave his own name and address to the boat-yard. Then, at the end of the trip, *he phones for his chauffeur!* What sort of madness was that, from a long-sighted man like Lammas?

'That's where I started going wrong. He had me fooled with the telephone call. Instead of accepting it and drawing an inference, I began looking for an accomplice in the family, somebody who could have traced Lammas to Ollby and then tipped off Hicks.

'And I didn't have to look very far. Both Mrs Lammas and Paul were absent from "Willow Street" at the time of the murder and neither of them had an alibi. What was more, their comings and goings were oddly mixed up with one another's – especially by the row at the end of them! As for motive, that's always a tricky business. You and I know, if judges don't, that nobody's quite sane when they come to do a murder. Mrs Lammas was the predatory type of woman who never lets go of the people she gets in her power. Paul Lammas had National Service hanging over his head – with his father standing by to kick him well and truly into it! To this you had to add their relation to Hicks. He was a confidential retainer whom either might influence. And when it came to finance, they had that too.

'Hicks, of course, was the perfect tool. We know more about him from Lammas' statement. He was a spy, a liar and what you might call Mrs Lammas' creature – Lammas suspected he was something more, but we've no proof of that. At all events, he'd been a wedge between them. Lammas hated him and he hated Lammas. I got enough of this out of the early interrogations to convince me that Hicks was a likely man.

'To complete the picture, there was the shadow of a fourth person – I made a certain pass at Mrs Lammas and her reaction suggested I was on the right track. We know now who it was, but then it was just something to be kept in mind. And it was the same with Linda Brent. She wasn't really impressive as a candidate for the murder of the man she loved, so . . . I'd just keep her in mind and see what turned up.

'Now the first thing to get at was whether Mrs Lammas or her son knew what Lammas was up to and the second – this was vital – whether they knew where to find him. But I was so much impressed by the oddness of that trip on the yacht that I felt compelled to tackle it before anything else. Unless I could get a reason for it, I felt I should miss the significance of other things which might turn up. And I was right . . . though it isn't much comfort to me.

'At the time my investigation of the trip seemed a complete waste of energy. I learned nothing of the motive for it except that it apparently had none. Lammas had behaved exactly as holidaymakers do behave. He had visited the same places, done the same things as the others, and it didn't seem to have worried him that he might have been recognized. His only departure from routine was when he went up Ollby Dyke – to get murdered! There was nothing else remarkable about the whole itinerary.

'Well, I ought to have seen it. I could kick myself now for *not* seeing it. Rouse . . . Tetzner . . . Saffran and Kipnik – I'd studied all their trials at one time or another. And yet I was still in the dark! Lammas had really pulled the wool over my eyes. And just to keep me well off the trail, I happened on some of the evidence I was looking for relating to Mrs Lammas.

'If only people wouldn't lie to the police!

'The next morning I was hard at it, proving that Mrs Lammas knew what her husband was trying to do. I had just succeeded in doing that when I heard about Annie Packer.'

Gently broke off, ostensibly to fill his pipe. But the super was well aware of the reason for that delicately-timed little pause. He shrugged his shoulders deprecatingly.

'I suppose I ought to apologize . . .'

'Admittedly, I was being a fool.'

'You couldn't have saved Annie Packer.'

'No, even Lammas couldn't have foreseen . . .'

'And I should know you better by now!'

Gently lit his pipe forgivingly. A gesture was all he asked for. He breathed a long stream of smoke into the darkening room and prepared to take up his tale again.

'Anyway – it brought me up with a jolt!

'It needed a fantastic theory to cover it. If Hicks had been the tool he must have been packed off into hiding – they wouldn't have left him dodging about the neighbourhood. And if someone else had done it, then it could only have been for a blind . . . but what sort of blind was this, which involved the murder of an innocent person? People don't kill so lightly, not even people with blood on their hands. There were a dozen ways short of murder to make us think that Hicks was still around – and all of them a good deal less risky.

'Yet murder had been done. Right there, on my very doorstep. And to make it artistically right, somebody had circulated a rumour of Hicks having been seen there before the murder took place.'

'Of course, we know now there was no connection,' the super interrupted. 'The rumour was Lammas' red herring. Packer's murder was purely fortuitous.'

Gently nodded.

'We know it now . . . but we didn't guess it then. I could see it only as an incredibly cold-blooded manoeuvre. And it seemed to indicate that somebody

236

was getting scared, very scared indeed – a fact which pointed in only one direction.

'But before going into that I had to learn what I could about Annie's killing. There were several curious points connected with it, not the least being the one you noticed about the origin of that rumour. How *could* it have been started by a stranger in a place like Upper Wrackstead? Everyone knew everyone, and strangers drew attention. Yet if a stranger hadn't done it then a native must have done . . . or else somebody actually *had* been seen who might have been taken for Hicks.

'You can judge how far I was out of my depth. I actually accepted the latter alternative – at least as a working hypothesis. I was so taken up with the idea of Mrs Lammas and Paul being in on it that I was looking at everything from their angle . . . you don't know how hard it is for me to admit that.'

Dutt cleared his throat sympathetically. *He* knew how hard it was!

'But to get back to the killing.

'Up to a point, I could reconstruct it. I could understand how Annie slipped out to visit Thatcher, how she was intercepted on the way, how she was shot with a silenced revolver and how her body was disposed of. What I couldn't understand was the absence of blood-stains. There had to be some, unless she'd been shot where she would fall into the Dyke. But that would have made a splash and there wasn't any splash – so there had to be some blood . . . and there wasn't any blood!

'Looking at it now, I can't think how I could have been so dense. Certainly, I got part of an answer when

237

I discovered that the wounded head had been bandaged. But the major fact was unexplained – some blood had been shed somewhere – and it was sheer, blind prejudice that stopped me from going to the right spot. You see, I was assuming that Annie's killer came from outside. He had waited for a victim to emerge, and *of course* Annie was shot *on the bank*. Was there ever such a classic example of an investigator preferring a theory to a fact?'

The super frowned uneasily at his blotter. He'd harboured a theory or two himself in this case.

'I don't see what else you could have thought at the time,' he observed cautiously.

'I could have followed that fact up. The answer wasn't far away. If I'd been on top of the situation just then we might have arrested Lammas twenty-four hours sooner than we did.'

The super held his peace. It wasn't entirely displeasing to hear Gently admit himself at fault. At the same time, he couldn't help feeling that Gently aimed at impossibly high standards in criminal investigation . . .

'Then there was the stub of greasepaint liner that I picked up off the rubbish-heap. Naturally, I was too bemused to see the significance of that right away. It seemed to connect somewhere. The Lammases were mixed up with amateur dramatics. But all I could think of was that Paul may have got hold of some of his sister's greasepaint and doctored himself to pass for Hicks . . . he *could* have dropped that stub out of his pocket while he was busy with Annie Packer.

'Anyway, I went after Paul in the best way I could, which was by showing him how near his mother stood to a murder charge. That took me to Marsh, and probably to the truth of what went on on Friday night. Only I didn't know it was the truth . . . and it might so easily not have been. At that point I was almost ready to back the Paul-Marsh-Mrs Lammas combination. It seemed too tempting to pass over. We hadn't got enough proof, and it might take some digging up, but we hadn't quite exhausted the possibilities – and there's such a thing as luck.

'And then I was checkmated again. Dutt, here, found us Linda Brent. We picked her up – you know what happened. It seemed past doubt that Linda Brent had guilty knowledge of *l'affaire* Lammas. And if she had, or even thought she had, then what became of a conspiracy which couldn't have been hatched till just before the murder? No – it went back further! It must have been plotted before Mrs Lammas discovered what her husband was doing and probably before the trip on the *Harrier*.

'There was the further factor of Miss Brent being in love with whoever she supposed did it. This seemed to point to Paul, and certainly Paul might have got at Hicks *after* he had paid his visit to "High Meadows". But how could Paul have planned what took place on Friday *in advance*?'

'This Brent woman might have let him know what his old man was up to,' suggested the super, intrigued.

'Yes – as far as the trip went. But how could she have known that Lammas would go up Ollby Dyke in such a convenient way, setting her off first at Halford Quay?'

'She might have been able to fix it . . .'

Gently nodded eagerly.

'That's where I began to smell the scent again. Because I couldn't think of one single way in which she or any of the others could have fixed such a thing!'

He eased back on his chair to give them time to appreciate the proposition. It was clear enough now, when one knew the denouement!

'You've got to remember how Lammas was placed. He'd cut his ties with his past, there was nothing there for a motive. It wasn't his business or his family which could draw him into a secret rendezvous. And if it wasn't these, what was it? What else could have been used to get him up Ollby Dyke just as he was about to fade away?

'There isn't an answer, but there is a corollary. If Lammas wasn't enticed up the dyke, then he must have gone there on his own initiative – and if that was the case, *who could have known he was there*?

'Mrs Lammas couldn't. She only knew he had set out towards Wrackstead. Paul couldn't. He didn't even know as much as that! And as for Marsh, he only knew what Mrs Lammas told him.

'Lammas was the only one who could have phoned Hicks and told him to come to Ollby Dyke.'

'You're forgetting Linda Brent,' the super interrupted. 'She may have known about Ollby Dyke and tipped Paul off.'

'No.' Gently shook his head. 'Paul couldn't have been tipped off. If he'd known what he was going to do, he'd have fixed the chauffeur before he left. He didn't need to phone unless his father *hadn't* arrived at Ollby, which was not the case.

'I'd got to this stage last night when we brought in Linda Brent. It still wasn't making sense, in fact I seemed to be back at the beginning again. If nobody else was involved, then Hicks must have killed him for the money . . . and if Hicks had done that, he was at once the cleverest, stupidest and luckiest criminal I had ever had to do with. In addition to which Linda Brent was violently in love with him!

'It was a round dozen of contradiction. I knew I must be seeing it cock-eyed. And it only seemed to make matters worse when I saw the cap and jacket and heard about the shack in the carrs . . .

'For instance, why would Hicks leave them there, of all places, when he might have stuffed them in the next ditch? If he'd been hiding there himself it would have been a reason. But you could tell me there were no signs of the shack being inhabited and an intensive manhunt had failed to turn up Hicks . . . so what was it all about? And as you asked me, if Hicks was around, where *was* he?

'I did the only thing I could think of. I cooked a charge against Linda Brent. If she were right about what she knew then it ought to worry someone, and a murderer getting worried has been known to put a foot wrong.

'Next, I was interested in the shack. It was too handy for Upper Wrackstead . . . and it did occur to me that Annie might have been lured aboard a dinghy.'

Gently broke off a little hoarsely. He wasn't used to speaking at such length. And his pipe kept going out, with all this persistent monologue.

241

'Is there any coffee left?'

The super kindly poured him some. It was cold and tasted of grounds, but it slaked a thirsty throat. Outside some stars were sparkling and the traffic was getting thin. Hansom was deciding to risk a cigar, even though he didn't come from the Central Office.

'I had a hunch about that shack.'

Gently's pipe was going again.

'I felt it would make or break me – I'd got into that state of mind! At first it looked like the latter, though I discovered a couple of things you'd missed. One of them suggested that a dinghy had been kept there, and the other that somebody had been using the place long before last Friday. But that didn't ring a bell. The dinghy fitted a surmise, the other simply added to the mystery.

'I stood in the shack by the nettles literally wrestling with those facts. I knew there must be a right way of seeing them and that I'd got the wrong way. I thought back over everything I'd done, everything which had come to light – odd little things, like the way Lammas had changed his shirt, or the way the jerrican disappeared from the garage, or the way we only found his and Mrs Lammas' prints on the gun-drawer. And always there loomed up the incredible folly of that week on the *Harrier* – against so much careful planning, so much able implementation! And after it the dismissal of Linda Brent to her hideaway and the inexplicable rendezvous at Ollby Quay.

'Just there, my mind seemed to be wandering. It kept reverting back to an interview I'd had with your County

Drama Organizer. Every time my ideas seemed to be building up to something my thoughts slipped away to that smiling little man and whatever it was he was trying to tell me.

'Psychology is a curious business. I'm tempted to think that had the solution worked out in my unconscious when I got that hunch about the shack ... Anyway, I discovered the local reason why my mind kept slipping – I was looking straight at a strip of paper which had been torn from a carmine greasepaint liner! And then I had it, all in a flash. From then on it was simply a bit of routine. There's a lot of mystery about a substitute corpse when you don't know what it is ... once you do, the murderer hasn't got much time ahead of him.'

Gently broke off again, as though that, for him, was the end of the matter. Routine was routine ... no need to go into that. The interest lay in how you got to your man.

'Here, but wait a minute!'

The super thought otherwise.

'Put the light on, somebody ... we don't have to sit here in the dark!'

Dutt obediently rose to his feet and a glare of fluorescence flooded the bare office. Gently screwed up his eyes and puffed a disapproving cloud of smoke.

'Did you know he was masquerading as Thatcher, right there on the spot?'

The stars had been ousted from their oblique wedge of sky.

'He was so damned good at it ... I had doubts even then.'

'But you had Thatcher in mind?'

'Of course. The date almost clinched it.'

'Dates? What dates, man?'

'Easter, principally . . . That was when Lammas put his plan in operation – he gives you the reason: it was then when his Society fixed the date of their conference. Having got that, he went to work. He booked the yacht and rented the bungalow . . . and started disappearing on mid-week trips. And at Easter Thatcher drifted into Upper Wrackstead Dyke, complete with a frowzy old houseboat and an alibi for being there only occasionally . . .'

'His widow!' grunted Hansom, whose memory had been stirred. 'And he was away Friday evening – we heard that right at the beginning.'

'Yes . . . we heard it from Annie Packer. There's an odd twist, if you like.'

'Then you knew it was Thatcher when you borrowed his dydle?'

The super was going to have it, one way or the other.

'I told you . . . I wasn't quite sure. And I had to prove my theory. I suppose I might have grabbed Thatcher on suspicion and established his identity, but there was just a chance it was someone else . . . I like to prove before I move.'

'I don't see what proof it was against Thatcher, your finding Hick's denture in the mud.'

'The denture wasn't.' Gently shot a wry glance at Dutt. 'But the bullets were.'

'Eh?'

'They might as well have had his signature on them. Only Thatcher knew what I was up to. There wasn't a soul about when I borrowed his dydle . . . it had to be Thatcher with the gun.'

'It was an unnecessary risk, Gently!'

'I didn't know he'd chase after us on the next bus.'

'A fine mess we'd have been in if he'd knocked off the pair of you.'

'No doubt he was thinking the same when he saw us with the denture . . .'

The holy of holies was silent for a space. Four tired policemen pursued their thoughts at their respectively salaried levels. Gently wondered if he would smoke again and decided that he wouldn't. He'd run out of peppermint creams while Lammas was making his statement.

'But why did the bloody fool *do* it?' exclaimed the super at last. 'He might just have faded away – nobody would have looked too hard to find him.'

'You're forgetting his wife . . . *she* would have looked.'

'It isn't motive enough!'

'Yes . . . when you remember how he loathed Hicks. But she was the cause of it. She pushed him over. It's the cold-hearted ones who menace society.'

'The cold-hearted ones!' The super mused over the phrase. 'You can't make that criminal. I suppose you wish we could?'

Gently's head shook slowly. 'They're not to blame either. They didn't choose themselves. Society's crude, you know . . . it's a brutal piece of work! All we've achieved so far is done with force . . . there must be other and better ways of living together.'

'"Christ knows!"' the super quoted.

'Christ knew – but society didn't.'

'We were just a lot of policemen – that's what he was trying to say. We wouldn't understand – the jury wouldn't understand – the judge wouldn't, either. It was only Christ he stood a chance with.'

'You're leaving out the hangman!'

Hansom wasn't soft with killers.

Gently shrugged his bulky shoulders. 'Christ might understand him, too!'

The money was under the floorboards in the houseboat and in the cracks of the same floorboards they found deposits of blood under deposits of soap-sud. The bullet that killed Annie had been removed, but a freshly puttied hole in one of the cabin doors showed where it had lodged.

Along with the money was a black japanned tin containing Lammas' make-up outfit. It was an expensive collection with numerous etceteras. There were two sticks of carmine liner, one of them virgin and unused.

The tin was contained in a waterproof bag, since neither the space under the floorboards nor the shack in the carrs had been dry situations. It had spent nearly three months in that shack while Lammas was leading his double life. It had been cached amongst the nettles along with Thatcher's paunch and costume. It was in the same cache that the blood-stained jacket and cap had been found . . . Lammas had donned them after the murder in case he was seen driving away the Daimler.

'I'm going to cadge a day out of this!'

Gently had finished his report at last.

'They had our Sunday, didn't they? Well, they owe me a day's fishing!'

He folded up the report and shoved it into an envelope. Dutt glanced at him apprehensively – he knew Gently's state of mind when his chief wanted to score off authority.

'Daresay they'd let you have it, sir, wevver they knows about it or not.'

'I don't care a damn if they would, Dutt. I'm going to have it, and they can go to hell!'

He threw the report down on Mrs Grey's parlour table and stalked over to the window. There were vacant moorings in the Dyke where the houseboat had been towed away.

'And I'm not going to buy a licence, Dutt!'

'No, sir. You won't buy a licence.'

'I'm just in the mood to talk to some river police – I should enjoy a little bit of prosecution!'

'Make you feel like a civvy, sir.'

'Yes, Dutt – it'd redress the balance!'

Still the sun was burning down, the last sun of June. On the dreamily throbbing hire boats they were reading of the murder. The biggest thing since Christie! 'Gently Arrests A "Murdered" Man.' Lammas was a myth already . . . he'd stopped being human when they clipped on the handcuffs.

'On second thoughts . . .'

Dutt waited. Gently often had second thoughts.

'Let's catch the next train back to town – I'm fed up with this part of the world!'

Dutt grinned at his superior. How many times had it happened like that? Gently's kicking never lasted – that was Chief Inspectorial nature.

'It'll be shocking hot in the city, sir.'

'I know. But never mind.'

'And I reckon we've missed the express—'

'I'd like to sweat on a stopper!'

His eyes met the Cockney sergeant's. For a moment he couldn't react. Then he grinned back and shrugged, and patted Dutt's burly arm.

'Come in and see the kids, sir,' said Dutt sympathetically, 'you'd be surprised the way they grow!'

Gently nodded. 'I think I'll do that. It's a mistake, my being a bachelor.'